CW00435628

This book is dedicated to all the people who run animal rescues around the world to pull creatures big and small from the edge of darkness and back into the light. It is dedicated to people who save bunnies like Jan Widdows Rebmann of the House Rabbit Society Chicago and Jennifer Macbeth of the South West Florida House Rabbit Rescue. It is also dedicated to Tina Garrett and Matt Venaleck of the South West Florida Horse Rescue for their work in saving horses and offering Werner a final resting place.

I must also thank my inspiration for this work, my partner in crime, Sharon Miller. I can think of no one who loves bunnies more.

A special thanks to Carolyn Reeve Ellicott who created the painting of Werner for the cover. It is her first creation and it is amazing.

Copyright 2021

ISBN: 9798745338014

All rights reserved. No part of this publication may be reproduced, distributed, or transmitted in any form or by any means, including photocopying, recording, or other electronic or mechanical methods, without the prior written permission of the publisher, except in the case of brief quotations embodied in critical reviews and certain other noncommercial uses permitted by copyright law.

HOW IT ALL BEGINS

I lie in silence as I await what will be my final sunrise, my final day in the light of this place. I can see the first ambassadors of the new day crawling over the horizon. The light in the sky grows stronger, as the light in my body begins to fade.

It is only now at the end of this journey, that I think about the beginning. About that moment when the cold, darkness gave way to a tiny ray of yellow light. How I slowly moved forward until I was immersed in the brilliance of a whole brand-new world.

I remember it being cold and very noisy when I first arrived. The previous 31 days had been spent in the darkness, silence, warmth, peace and security only a mother can provide. Now, out in the world I could hear many new sounds and smells but could not see at first because of the light and the fluids on my eyes.

I am not sure when I became aware I was a rabbit. I was born in a barn with my 8 brothers and sisters. We all looked the same, white and fuzzy with red eyes that changed to a beautiful purple in just the right light.

When my eyes cleared, I started to look around and see animals in different shapes and sizes. There were cows and pigs, chickens and goats. It was a dazzling display of color and sound, part of a majestic quilt.

My mom told me every animal in the barn had a purpose to the farmer who watched over and cared for us. The cows and goats gave milk. The chickens provided eggs. The horses would work the fields. The dogs would fight off predators. The cats had their job dealing with the mice who liked to overindulge in the farmer's grain.

When I asked what my purpose was, my mom hesitated before saying, "Your purpose is to bring joy to the world. You are made to make people laugh when they are sad, comfort them when they feel lonely and remind them it is the simple things in life which bring us the most happiness."

"How can I do all of that?" I asked.

"By just being yourself," Mom replied. "You are one of a kind. There is no one else like you. You are one piece in the grand creation and like a piece in a puzzle, you fit where God intended."

In the days following my arrival into this new world I learned a great deal about my place in it. In the first few days we were not allowed outside the little pen we were born in. Mom said there were creatures out there that were dangerous and could do us harm.

The days went by quickly and I grew bigger and stronger every day. Each day my mom would lecture me and my siblings about the world around us.

She taught us about the fox, the hawk and the other animals hunting us from the ground and from the air, ready to turn us into a meal. She also taught us about the animals in nature that were our friends. I was wary of the danger outside the barn but anxious to explore the sights and sounds beyond the doors. She taught us to respect all life, big and small. She said there was no more important rule, for life was so very precious.

On a hot summer day, my mom came to me and said it was time to make my first trip outside the barn. She had taken each of my brothers and sisters out one at a time to teach us about our new home. It was now my turn. I was excited and afraid all at once.

"Stay close by and if danger stalks, run right back here," she ordered.

"Yes ma'am."

And with that, we were off running and hopping through the green grass and amazing fields of flowers. I would hop and twist in the air to take it all in mindful all the time that danger could be around the next turn.

She took me on a tour of the magnificent fields surrounding the farm showing me what things we could eat and what things we needed to avoid. Green leafy veggies were okay, mushrooms were not. Bunny food was good, most human foods were not. Though she admitted many human treats were indeed tasty.

We learned how to find water, how to stay warm and how to build a den. We learned how to spot the long list of predators both on the ground and in the air.

We had been out only a few minutes when I spotted something that looked very out of place in a field of sunflowers. My ears opened like satellite dishes and I stood up to scan the horizon, stretching as high as I could go. At first, all I could see was a brown and fluffy object. As I scanned down, I finally spotted the head of a fox, lurking in the patch.

Mom had warned me that if I had spotted any danger, I should not hesitate to head back to the barn. My paws and teeth would be no match for such a nasty predator. But it was already too late.

In a flash, the fox was on me and I took flight to escape. But in the chaos, I was not sure which direction to go in, so I just ran. I ran until I felt my heart and lungs would burst from my chest. I dug into a clump of bushes to avoid the pursuit and watched as the fox raced by.

I waited for a long time before deciding to move. When I could hear nothing but the wind and crickets, I decided I could come out of hiding. It took me a while but I finally found my way back to the barn.

But when I arrived the door was closed and there was no apparent way in. I clawed at the door and whispered "mom" so as not to draw too much attention to myself. The fox was a crafty creature and I could not be sure if he was listening at that very moment for me to reveal myself.

The light was fading as the sun began to set. I knew nighttime was no time for a baby bunny to be out in the open. After a few minutes, I heard a scratch from the other side and instructions to head around the side of the barn. There I was greeted by a baby pig who showed me a small hole that I was able to squeeze through.

"Thank you so much," I said as I wiggled safely back inside the barn.

"No problem," the pig said. "I once used the same hole to go out for walks."

"But now," he said, motioning to his ever-growing belly, "I can't make it through anymore, even if I hold my breath."

We both laughed and I thanked him for his help before heading back to the corner of the barn where I found my mom and our family.

"Where have you been?" Mom asked with great concern.

"A fox chased me," I replied.

"Yes, I saw him. Are you okay?"

"He never even got close mom. I zigged and zagged, jumped and waggled," I cried out, replaying every moment of the chase.

"You may not be so lucky the next time," she said giving me a big fat furry hug. "The world can be a very dangerous place for a bunny. Especially a little one like you. Remember you are only lucky until your luck runs out, only the fastest animal in the world until someone faster catches you."

My brothers and sisters were anxious to hear about my great adventure and hung on every word as I told the story. I could see the fear in their faces at every turn and the smiles at the end when I told them how the baby pig had let me back in the barn.

I fell asleep that night dreaming of the adventure and feeling like I was indeed the fastest and most clever animal in the world.

A MOTHER'S WISDOM

Every child has a moment in their life with their mom they will never forget. Mine came on a warm and sunny spring morning. Mom grabbed me by the fur and took me out into the garden. We were alone, which meant this was important. Usually, mom would bring us all out together. This time it was just me and her.

She motioned for me to come lie next to her in a patch of grass.

"Close your eyes," she said as we basked in the sun. "Can you feel it? The light, the warmth, the hand of God reaching out to you, embracing you. Take a deep breath and let it all in."

I closed my eyes and took a deep breath. I didn't feel anything at first.

"Relax," mom said. "Let it in."

I twisted and turned, trying to find just the right spot in the grass, the right position for my body. I felt bad that nothing was happening.

"I don't feel anything," I finally said.

"You will, relax, try to think of something that makes you happy," she replied.

I started to think of all the wonderful things around me, my family, the other animals around me, the flowers, the trees. And then slowly I could feel something sweep over me.

I could start to sense what mom was talking about. I could feel the natural world embrace me. I was at peace, no fear, no thoughts of the outside world, only a feeling of being part of something bigger.

"The light stays in your heart from your first breath until your last," mom whispered. "It is always there for you. It will give you comfort when you are afraid, when you alone, when you are sick and when your time here is over."

"And the light will teach you the most important lesson of all, never envy another, never wish to be something other than what you are. There is no greater sin. God created you with a purpose. You are a rabbit and shall live your best life as one. Do not envy the bird that can fly, the fish that can swim or the creatures capable of grand song. You are the rabbit and you are special every moment you take a breath."

"The warmth of the sun will comfort you on cold days and through rough times. It will be there when no one else is."

And that is how we spent the afternoon, basking in the sunlight, drifting between the conscious world and a dream state. It was a place of great joy and happiness where I felt safe. It was the first time I really knew what it felt to be alive and a part of something larger than myself.

In the days that would follow and the months after that, I would enjoy my moments in the sun. It was always my refuge.

Life went on with a simplicity and joy about it until the day the farmer entered the barn with a stranger we had never seen. He was all dressed in black with a hooded sweatshirt. He also wore a green hat that read Pet Kingdom. He had on boots that had a very worn look about them. And he had a dirty smell about him, even for a human. You could smell the fear in the barn as he entered. All of the animals inside could sense no good could come of him.

The farmer and the man approached our pen. The stranger reached in and tried to grab me but I was easily able to escape. His hand then roamed the cage until he settled in on my sister Ruth, the slowest of our colony.

He picked her up and gave her an exam just like the veterinarian the farmer brought in from time to time. But this exam had a different purpose.

"Florida whites," the farmer broke in. "A hearty breed. They are all in good health. They make great pets and of course can be used for a number of other things. "

I had learned from mom that "other things" meant eating. I found it hard to believe that humans would eat rabbits but I had learned from other animals in the barn that humans would indeed eat just about anything, even each other.

The stranger gave Ruth a good look. She offered little resistance since she was a kind and innocent creature not well versed in the dangers of the human world. She was unaware her life was about to change in a big way.

"Okay," the stranger said. "$150 for the lot."

"Sorry," the farmer replied. "I need to be at $200 on this lot.

The man looked inside his wallet, rubbed his jaw and looked once more at the creatures before him. He then nodded yes.

My brother Jacob and I were loaded into one cage. Ruth and the rest of my brothers and sisters went into another. There did not appear to be any reason why we were separated the way we were. We were all loaded into an old, broken-down truck and off to our next destination.

"Where are we going?" Ruth asked in a frightened voice.

"We are going to new homes," I said in a reassuring voice.

"But I like our home. What about mom?" she began to cry.

"Mom will be there waiting for us when we find out way back."

Mom had taught me never to lie. But in this case, I thought a lie was required. A wise old owl in the barn had once said to me, "sometimes a lie is required to allow someone time to realize a truth they cannot see and that will eventually come to them when they are better prepared for it."

I could see the look of fear on the faces of my brothers and sisters. A sense of sadness began to sweep over me as I realized we would never gather in the barn together again as a family. Never play and run around together in the garden. Never sleep in a big pile of fur on a cold night to stay warm. Never be together with mom as she told us bedtime stories and grand tales of the world beyond the farm.

The truck sputtered and coughed as it rumbled down the road. I thought it might even break down and allow us a chance to escape.

But 20 minutes into the ride the truck came to a sudden stop. The air was cold as a woman in a grey dirty dress opened the door, reached in and grabbed the cage with my five brothers and sisters.

"These will do," she said to the man. "They look very healthy and well-fed."

I knew from the look in the eyes of my siblings they realized it would be the last time we would ever see each other. A tear filled my eye and I rubbed it away with my paw, trying to remain strong for the others.

It broke my heart that I would never know their fate. Would they find good homes or end up in bad circumstance? I would certainly think of them every day and pray they would have the chance to live a good bunny life.

After the woman gave the driver some money the truck resumed its journey with Jacob and I still wondering what would become of us. A short time later we pulled up to a large building with a green and blue sign that read Pet Kingdom.

Our cage was pulled from the truck and we were carried a short distance inside the building. Long before we were inside, we could smell the menagerie of animals awaiting us inside. And we could hear the different pieces of their chaotic symphony.

It wasn't until we came around the corner that we saw the enormous number of animals inside. It was a Noah's Ark of God's smallest creations. There were birds, snakes, fish, mice, cats and dogs. It was indeed a Kingdom of Pets.

Jacob and I were carried into an area near the front of the store where we were dropped into a glass enclosure with another rabbit. He had beautiful white fur with gray markings all across his body. He had floppy ears and seemed to be a rabbit of good character.

"Hello, I am Bini the Bunny," he said, approaching us in a cheerful greeting. "Welcome to the Kingdom."

"Where are we?" Jacob asked.

"You are in a pet store. Humans come in here looking for pets and if you are lucky one of them will pick you up and take you home."

"How long will we be here?" I asked.

"It depends. Some animals go fast, others have been here a while. Me, I got here last week. I am the last of a litter of 5. I guess the right person just hasn't come along yet to understand my unique personality. Oh, and the price tag on me is a little steep.

"Price tag?"

"Yes, they are asking $100 for me. But I think I am worth it."

"You guys will probably sell for around $50. Don't get me wrong, you are good-looking guys, you just ain't no Bini."

"How do we eat?" I asked.

"They will come around twice a day. Once after the sun comes up, once after the sun goes down. We get lettuce, carrots, hay, some protein pellets and water. The basics. It's not bad but it is the same thing every day. It gets pretty boring. And this ain't no barn so if nature calls go over in that litter box so it doesn't get all over. They come and clean it every other day."

"Litter box?" I asked.

"Yes, it's a way humans train animals so they don't make a mess all over."

"Is there any way to escape this place?"

"Escape? To where? Look outside. We wouldn't last five minutes out there with all the city stuff, the people and the predators?"

"City stuff?"

"Yes, there are all sorts of bad things that can happen to you in a city. You could get run over by a car, hit by a bus, smashed by a garbage truck. And of course, if you do escape into the countryside, you might encounter a hunter or two. Me, I am taking my chances on someone nice coming to take me home."

Bini went on giving us a rundown of how things at the pet store worked. We took it all in.

About an hour later a nice-looking young girl came by and dumped some food into our cage. She filled our water dishes and gave each of us a little rub on the head and a kind word. She was gone just as quickly as she appeared.

We divided the food up into three equal portions and went about the business of eating. Jacob and I hadn't had anything to eat all day because we were taken so early in the morning from the barn.

Bini laughed as Jacob and I inhaled our food and drank heartily from the water dishes. I was in the middle of a good bunny cleaning when the overhead lights in the store went out.

"Good night everyone," the girl called out as she walked out. "Sleep tight, don't fight. Tomorrow could be your lucky day."

"She says that every night," Bini said. "I thought she was nuts the first time she did it but it is actually good advice."

"Now what?" I asked.

"Well, now you are supposed to go to sleep even though we are crepuscular animals. That means we are most active at dawn and dusk. I always wondered why the pet shop wasn't open when we were most active. I mean who wants to buy a bunch of sleepy animals."

Jacob and I curled up together to keep warm and for comfort in this strange new place. We invited Bini over but he resisted at first, trying to play the tough guy.

"Sure, if it makes you guys feel better," he said as he finally joined us in a big pile of fur. Bini was a good fit for the pile. There is nothing more comforting and peaceful than a sleeping pile of bunnies.

I worried that it would be tough sleeping in this place though with all the pumps, lights, singing, barking and howling that went on all night. But I finally gave in to sleep, exhausted from the day we had endured and nervous about the days ahead.

OUR NEW HOME

Mom told me tomorrow always comes, it just doesn't come for everyone. If you are lucky to greet the new day, embrace it as a grand gift and don't waste a moment of it. And that is how I greeted the new day in the pet shop. Who knew what adventure the day might bring?

Well, the new day brought nothing and neither did the day after or the day after that. In fact, the days began to blend together. One the same as the next.

We would be fed and cleaned. Humans would come in to give us a look. Some might pick us up and play with us, giving rise to hope we might be going to a new home. Then they would put us back and the waiting would resume.

Some would terrorize us by pounding on the glass of our cage or shaking it. Humans could be cruel. Mom had warned us about this species of man. She called terrorizing another living creature for sport a sin. She told us never to steal the dignity of another living creature. It would make God sad and damage our soul.

Other humans would just come and look, comment on how cute we looked. The child would say, "Please dad, I want…" And the father would immediately reply, "No," in a loud and strong voice.

It would usually be followed by phrases like, who is going to take care of it, you are too young, it is too expensive. The child would then respond with a long list of false promises. The father would end the debate by saying things like, maybe for your birthday, for Easter, for Christmas, or whatever other occasions that would get dad off the hook.

We were generally treated well at the pet shop. The young girl who cared for us would occasionally stop and play with us and from time to time drop some new toys into the cage for us to play with. I particularly enjoyed this plastic ball she dropped in the cage that was filled with pellets. You pushed the ball and the pellets came falling out. It was nice.

We started to lose track of bunny time. It was hard to tell when to sleep, when to wake up. When to eat, when to poop. I stopped trying to figure out where one day ended and the next one began. Animals would go out the front door with their new human owners and be replaced by new ones coming in through the back.

I was half asleep when a little girl by the name of Sarah approached our pen. Sarah was maybe 7 or 8 in human years and just tall enough to see into our pen. She had a pretty yellow bow in her blonde hair, a blue sweater and a green dress.

She first looked through the glass to give us a look over. We all turned toward her and struck a pose, hoping to win her favor. Perhaps if we looked cute enough, she would take all three of us home. I must say I was a bit excited when she pointed at me.

"That one," she said to her dad. "I like that one dad. He is so cute."

The man working the floor that morning picked me up and placed me in her arms.

"Careful," he said. "This is a real bunny. Not a toy."

Sarah was quite gentle as she held me but the experience left me a bit shaken. I did not sense a great deal of strength in her body and it was a long way to the floor. I kept thinking; I am not a bird.

"Can I get him, dad? Please?"

"Okay, but only if you promise, double and triple promise that you are going to take care of him. You heard the man; this is a real live bunny. He is not a toy. You need to feed him, give him water, clean him and play with him."

"Yes, daddy,' she said with a voice even I could recognize as the sound that comes from someone when they are making a false promise.

The store clerk went over the instructions for the care and feeding of a rabbit. I did not realize I was so needy as they started to pile up all the supplies, they would need to care for me. I wanted to tell that that I was quite capable of taking care of myself.

There was a cage, food, bowls, a litter box, litter, hay, toys and the dreaded water bottle. I hated water bottles. I was raised on a farm where real rabbits drank from rivers, streams and puddles left behind by rain. They were also given the name of a veterinarian who would give me medical care and take care of anything else I needed if I got sick.

I could see Jacob and Bini through the holes in my box and tried to wave goodbye. I was not sure if they could see my paw sticking out through the hole.

"That will be $245.76," the cashier said.

Wow, I thought. I am worth $245. The father reached into his wallet, handed the clerk a plastic card and just like that I had a new home.

I was beginning to think I was something special with all the humans spending so much on me. I must admit I was a bit nervous about where my new adventure would take me. I so hoped that they had a barn with other animals where I would live, just like where I came from.

The dad picked up the box and all my accessories and carried me out to a very large black car. They placed me in the back seat right next to Sarah. Her face was right against the box the entire trip just staring at me. From time to time, she tried to slip her finger into the box to pet my head.

The trip gave me plenty of time to think about where I was headed. I had heard in the barn that some humans would treat animals well, while others would not. You could find a home where the humans loved you, one where they just had you around like furniture or one where they abused or neglected you. I had high hopes for my new home.

The car finally came to a stop and I could hear Sarah and her father getting out.

"Let me bring all of this stuff in first," the father said, referring to long list of items they would need to care for me. "Then, I will come back for him. I want to let mom know we are back."

Sarah sat with me the entire time.

"Don't be afraid. You are going to love your new home. We are going to have so much fun together."

A few minutes later her father returned and picked me and the box up and carried us a short distance into the house I could see through the holes in the box. It was not a barn, but a massive brick building fit for a king.

They brought me inside and laid me down in the middle of a grand room. They opened the box and I moved to the opening to get my first look at my new surroundings.

My box was sitting on a large rug, which was good because my nails made navigating slippery surfaces difficult. There were all sorts of pictures and paintings on the walls. I took it as a good sign that there were pictures of animals and shots of nature in the collection.

It was the first time I had ever been inside the house of a human. There was grand furniture all about, much different than the barn back home. It also smelled very different from the barn and farm that I was used to. It smelled too clean and made me sneeze.

"Bless you," the mother said.

I looked up to see a lovely woman with blonde hair. She had a different smell than the farmer's wife and a much different appearance. She had a bow instead of a hat. She had on a dress instead of overalls and wore pretty shoes instead of boots. She looked just like Sarah. I only hoped that she would be as kind as the farmer's wife.

Then there was the man, dressed very differently than the farmer who once cared for me. He was dressed in rather fancy clothes and smelled much differently than the farmer. He smelled more like a flower than the earth it grew in.

"Come on little guy," the girl coaxed.

"Give him a minute Sarah," the father cautioned. "Let him get used to things."

I wasn't sure what to do. Mom had not told me how to act as a pet. I peeked my head out of the container I was in and was immediately greeted by the barking of a large dog. I knew from the farm that some dogs were friends and others meant me harm.

"Barney down," the father shouted. "Shut up."

The shouting only added to the anxiety I was feeling. Barney immediately obeyed and sat at attention.

He was large, brown shaggy and looked like a giant stuffed toy. Barney had signs of grey in his fur, telling me he had been around for some time and not only knew the rules of the house, but the ways of the world. He seemed to be a good fellow but you can never be too sure with dogs.

Out of the corner of my eye I could see three cats. Mom told me to never trust a cat because you could never know what side of the barn they woke up on any particular day. They also had the cat stare that made it hard to read what they were thinking. I saw no reason to trust them.

"Come out Werner," the little girl said again.

Werner, I thought to myself, what kind of crazy name was that. Mom had called me her little snowball because of my pure white fur. Animals didn't usually have names for each other. It just wasn't something we did.

"You are going to name your rabbit after grandpa?" the father asked.

"Yes. I think he would like that."

I would later learn that grandpa Werner had died a few weeks earlier. Sarah's parents hoped that her new pet would help her remember him and deal with his death. She had taken it hard.

I cautiously took my first steps into my new world feeling the eyes of everything and everyone on me. I stood up on my hind legs and deployed my ears to survey the landscape before me. I was not looking for the obvious but for the things humans cannot detect, a sound, a smell or another marker that would signal danger.

I was overwhelmed by the concerto of sounds. There were low-level hums, whirrs, buzzes and other noises that were foreign to this country bunny now living in the heart of the city.

I ventured further and further from the container just like the explorers taking their first steps on the moon. I had memories of my days in the field, looking up at the moon and wondering what it would be like to run around there. Mom told me no rabbits had ever been there. Now I knew what it must feel like to step foot on a foreign light in the sky.

I started to hop around the room, checking out all of the new terrains before me. There were things I had never seen before; smells I had never experienced. As I explored, I spotted a thin ribbon on the ground. Thinking it a snake I approached and was greet with a loud, "Noooooooo," by the entire family.

I would later find out it was an electric cord. It called to me. The hum inside kept saying, come bite me.

It was then I noticed the two young boys who were also part of the family. One was a little older than Sarah, the other was a year or two younger. They stood by with a rather amazed look on their faces. It seemed to be the first time they had seen a rabbit up close and in their own house.

We are going to have to police up all of these wires," the father cried out. "From what I have read these little guys love to chew wires and if we are not careful there won't be a working appliance in this house."

I could hear a low-level hum coming from the wires in front of me and thought it was something I would have to come back and check out in the future, especially since it had caused some concern for my new family. The sound was intoxicating.

After being given a few minutes to look around Sarah picked me up and carried me to where I would be spending most of my time. It was a small room just off the kitchen equipped with a cage, some fencing, a little box, a bowl of pellets, a dish for food and an odd-looking bottle hanging inside the cage.

It was everything a growing bunny could ask for, except for that bottle. I wasn't sure how any self-respecting bunny could drink out of it. How was I supposed to get water from this odd-looking contraption?

The family gathered around me and I could feel them looking down from above. It was almost as they were expecting me to fly, talk or perform some other amazing act. I nibbled a little at some of the food my new family had laid out. Not bad, it was fresh and it was a nice variety.

My area was surrounded by a fence. I wasn't sure if it was supposed to keep me in or keep danger out. It would not take me long to figure out that the family was concerned about all the mischief I could get into. They were of course right but how could they think anything that looked so cute could be so dangerous?

The fence was three feet high and would not be much of a challenge if I really wanted to escape. It would be no problem to jump over the top. Of course, I had already noticed the door on the fence was only locked by a cheap-looking latch that would be easily opened.

The family stood around my enclosure for some time waving odd toys in my face, calling out in strange voices and making annoying sounds as if I were a human baby. It was all designed to lure me into doing unnatural tricks. "Please, I am no common cat or dog," I thought. "I am a rabbit. We have our dignity."

"Okay, guys," the mom finally said. "Let's leave him be."

"Yes, leave me be," an excellent idea.

The light of the day began to fade and as the darkness fell outside a number of lights came on inside. There was a nightlight in the shape of a rabbit, perhaps to keep me company. The light was very bright. There was so much light that it wasn't very dark at all in the room.

I could hear the family in the other room talking and doing the sorts of things human families do. From time to time someone would come in to check on me. I would get an occasional pat on the head or a loving glance. Someone was always checking my water and food. It was fine at first but started to get annoying when I would try to grab a little nap and they kept waking me up.

I decided to check out the food that had been left for me. It was actually pretty good. There were a lot of fresh vegetables, nice sweet hay and even a few treats mixed in with it all. Overall, it was four-star chow.

A short time later I could hear the family had decided to call it a night and head off to bed. I decided that it was my cue to explore the world outside of my little compound. I made quick work of the latch to the cage, flipping it open with my nose and heading out into the house. It was dead silent except for the sounds coming from the machines going on and off in an odd rhythm. And there was of course the sound of my nails dancing across the wooden floors.

Instead of grass and brush, I found carpeting and furniture. The stars I was used to seeing in the sky at night were replaced by the artificial glow of man's machines. There were nightlights, clocks, appliances and security cameras. What came naturally to me, the warning signs of sound, smell, touch were all alien to humans.

They seemed to need their machines to help them find their way and protect them from the world. Mom told me it had not always been this way for humans. They were once like us, able to live in the real world with ease. It now seemed the more they tried to connect to the world through their machines, the more disconnected they became.

I wandered around the home exploring all the little nooks and crannies. I jumped up on the furniture, finding it very soft and an excellent place for a nap. The smell of dog and cat was everywhere. I would have to change that of course to mark my territory.

I was taking in the sights when I turned a corner and came face to face with the three cats I had seen earlier. I immediately thumped, forcing them to back away.

"That's no way to say hello," the large gray cat meowed.

"Sorry," I apologized. "You startled me and thumping is how I react sometimes. I mean you no harm. I just got here and was scoping the place out."

"Apology accepted. My name is Sparks," the gray cat went on, offering a more formal introduction. "Got the name because I burned up my tail chewing on some wires."

"This is Snowflake," he continued nodding toward the small white cat to his left. "Pretty obvious name there."

Obvious indeed for Snowflake was a pure white cat with fur that looked just like mine.

"And this is Kingdom," Sparks said motioning toward the large black cat to our right.

Kingdom was jet black except for white markings around his head that looked like a crown. It made him look like a king.

"I know nice names. But what can you do? Humans don't get that animals don't have names for each other. But it's kinda their thing. It could be worse we could have gotten stuck with names like Princess, Cupcake or God knows what else."

"Well, they are calling me Werner," I protested.

"It's not as bad as you think. The grandfather here was named Werner. He was a great guy. He would always sneak us treats, take us outside when we weren't supposed to and take care of us when we got sick. We miss him. Things changed a bit when he died."

"You will get plenty of attention for the first few weeks," Snowflake offered. "But after that, you start to blend into this drab routine and are left on your own. We take care of each other here."

"What about the dog?' I asked.

"Pain in the butt," Spark replied, "but he has a good heart. He just barks too much. He barks at birds, the mailman, the delivery man, just about anything that moves. It makes it hard to sneak around and get into any real trouble."

"Is he dangerous?" I asked.

"Not unless you are worried about getting licked to death," Kingdom said.

"The family is big on tricks," Sparks went on. "The more tricks you do, the more attention and treats you get."

"Snowflake here is big on the tricks," he said pointing toward his expanding girth.

"Yeah, so I could lose a few pounds," Snowflake fired back. "Couldn't we all?"

"Where do you sleep? They have me locked in a compound in the back."

"We sleep wherever we wish. Barney sleeps upstairs in the bedroom with the parents. They have you in the back because your kind has a reputation of eating wires and causing mischief at night."

"We were actually a bit concerned about what the family might be bringing home when we saw the large compound they were building," Snowflake added.

We thought maybe they were bringing in a Pitbull or a raptor. It was kinda scary all the work they did to get your little area prepared.

"Yes, I hear we have a bad reputation for eating things we aren't supposed to," I responded.

"How did you get out of your area so fast," Kingdom asked.

"It was a piece of cake. They built all of these high fences and security but the thing is locked with a cheap latch that is easy to flip up and open. It only took a minute or two to figure out how to open and close it."

Before I could go on, Snowflake bumped into a table and a book fell to the ground making a frightful noise. We began to hear a muffled bark from upstairs. The door to one of the upstairs bedrooms burst open and lights suddenly began to light up the area. Barney had sensed a disturbance in the force and decided to wake the entire family.

"Party's over kids," Sparks called out. Time for us to scatter and for you to get back home my friend."

"Indeed. We will talk again soon. Later, cats," I said as I headed off quickly toward my compound.

I turned to see my three new friends taking up poses around the room behind me. Sparks jumped up and assumed a sleeping position on a couch. Kingdom did the same under a table. And Snowflake flopped down in a bed 5 times his size. I assumed that it belonged to Barney. They all had innocent smiles on their faces.

As I scrambled back home, I could hear the father coming down the stairs shouting, "So, what in heaven's name is going on down here?"

I quickly re-entered my cage, closed the door and flipped the latch closed behind me. It magically clicked shut just as the main light in my room ignited, filling the room with a white glow.

As the father looked down on me in the cage, I raised my head off the ground and gave him a sleepy, confused look. I made it appear that I had been asleep for hours and was just now being awakened from a deep sleep.

"Nothing to see here," I whispered under my breath. "All is well."

After doing a quick survey of my area the father was satisfied that all was indeed well. He turned off the light and grabbed Barney by the collar, leading him away.

"You stupid dog, waking up everyone for nothing. What am I doing to do with you?"

I smiled in the darkness.

"Everything is fine," I could hear the father tell his wife. "This goofy dog is hearing things. Maybe we need to take him to the vet to have his hearing checked."

With that, the door to the room upstairs closed and the lights went out. A peaceful calm returned to the house.

I had enjoyed enough adventure for my first day so I decided to grab some sleep. It came quickly, along with dreams of my mom, my siblings and my days in the fields running and jumping as rabbits do.

TRIP TO THE ANIMAL DOCTOR

I woke up just as the rest of the house was rising for the new day. It was funny how a house full of humans could go from dead silent to the roar of a filled sports stadium in a matter of minutes.

Mom and dad were up first and that meant Barney barking to go out for his morning call of duty. After the father sent Barney outside, Mom than rustled the kids from their sleep and got them dressed. The father then started to make some breakfast for everyone.

It was a dizzying experience to watch it all unfold. There were plates and clothes and lunch bags and book bags all flying around. Everyone was talking at once and it was impossible to believe that anyone was really hearing what anyone else was saying. But there did seem to be a method to the madness.

The dad went flying out the door with the kids saying, "Remember the vet appointment is for 9 AM. They are squeezing Werner in as a favor."

"Got it," the mother replied. "I have all of his papers, carrying case and other stuff ready. See you guys at dinner."

And just like that the house fell silent again. Mom went about getting herself ready for the day and then turned her attention to me.

I had never been to an animal doctor or veterinarian as humans called them. All I knew about them was that they took care of animals when they got sick. Well, I wasn't sick so I wasn't sure why I was going anywhere.

She came walking up to me, talking that annoying baby talk as she tried to coax me into the carrying case she had sitting behind her. I do not understand why humans talk to animals like we are babies. We understand the many languages you speak, simply be clear and concise.

I think her plan was to grab me and throw me in. I simply ran around her and jumped into the case. There was no need for violence or a struggle.

The trip to the animal doctor only took a few minutes. I could tell we had arrived by all the smells and sounds coming from inside the building we had entered.

I wasn't exactly sure what I was in for but it did not take long to find out. Before I could even get my footing inside the carrying case, I was being pulled out by a woman dressed all in blue. She had on a blue top, blue pants, blue shoes and even a blue ribbon in her hair. There was no question she was in charge.

I was placed on to an ice-cold table. They could have at least put a towel down. It sent a shiver from my paws all the way up to my brain.

"Hey there, little guy. How are you doing?" she said picking me up and squeezing me just like the farmer back home checking to see if his crops were ready for market. She pried open my mouth to check my teeth. Checked my undercarriage, my paws and ears.

I would actually be doing much better I thought if you would stop squeezing me and putting hands where hands should not go.

"Looking good so far," she said. "Everything is where it should be. I see here that you want him fixed."

"Fixed? There was nothing broken. Why was I going to be fixed? The next thing I know I was getting a shot. The farmer never gave me shots. I never got shots at the pet store. No shots now."

I tried to resist as she approached with a long piece of metal which I was pretty sure was going into me somewhere. But out of nowhere a large human dressed in the same blue outfit appeared to restrain me. Resistance was futile as the army of blue humans restrained me and injected God knows what inside of me.

Before I knew it, I had fallen into a deep sleep. Everything seemed just fine until I woke up and discovered something very important was missing. My boy parts. I had grown rather fond of them and now they were suddenly gone.

There was no need for this. Animals have one job, to make more animals. I knew there were already too many bunnies out there without homes. But I lived alone after all. My girl options were very limited.

"He came through just fine. He will be a little groggy for a bit and may sleep for a few hours. But everything went well. Just make sure he gets fresh vegetables every day. Limit the amount of pellets. Treats are okay in moderation. Make sure there is plenty of water available and that he gets plenty of exercise. You need to interact with him on a regular basis to maintain his mental health as well."

"Okay, doctor. Thank you." The mother said.

With that I was given a tasty treat, a pat on the head and slipped back into my carrier. We were back home before I even knew what happened.

The woman dropped me from the carrying case back into my compound. I immediately retreated to the small house they had in the back where I could clean off the dirty oils and smells of the humans. They are actually rather dirty creatures. You rarely see them licking themselves to clean up after a meal or interaction with another human.

I would spend the rest of the afternoon napping and snacking. I kept looking down to the shaved spot where my boy parts had once been. The only bright spot, I might be able to run faster now.

THE DAILY ROUTINE

The world slowly slipped into a mind-numbing routine. I would wake up sometime just before dawn and wait until someone wandered in to feed me. There would be fresh lettuce, some carrots and maybe a little fruit. There was of course also a small bowl of pellets and a handful of hay.

Most of the time it was pretty good but there were days when I started to crave a little variety. I learned that begging didn't work. I would stand on my hind legs and give them a look that cried for a piece of banana, toast, anything that would break the cycle.

The worst were the days when they took the leftovers from the night before, mixed in whatever fresh stuff they could find and dropped it down in front of me. Someone had clearly forgotten to put bunny food on the list when they went to the store for their weekly food gathering.

Someone would come and clean my compound and change the pellets in my litter box two or three times a week. I was no fan of the litter box. I was used to answering the call of nature in nature. After a while it would start to smell so bad even I couldn't take it.

I get no one wants to clean the litter box but hey I can't do it. Maybe if you let me outside like Barney you wouldn't have this problem. Does anyone ever think about taking a bunny out for a walk?

Letting the litter box go uncleaned for too long was not only a bad idea for me, it was also a bad idea for the family. I could tell people were starting to avoid me. I could not blame them.

Just when I was thinking that I would lose my mind from the boredom, the pace of things jumped into high gear. It was clear that some big event was coming up.

The phones started to ring more. The conversations became more excited and agitated. The family was making lists, moving around tables and chairs, talking about food. It sounded like there was going to be a very big feast of some kind.

I very quickly became an afterthought. My food was now dumped on a plate and tossed into my cage instead of being placed there gently. No one talked to me or even bothered to throw a small toy or treat my way.

The top of my cage became a dumping ground for shopping bags, coats, book bags and just about anything that needed to be stored in a place that was "out of my way", the mother would command.

When people started to dump wet boots and coats into my area, I had to draw the line. I turned a $200 pair of Nikes into sandals one night, along with a $40 pair of mittens. That was the end of dumping shoes or any other chewables into my area.

I eventually learned that the big day approaching was something called Easter. It was the day a mythical creature called the Easter Bunny would come. Mom had never told me about this super rabbit that comes and brings candy, toys and all sorts of other things to children.

Most nights I would break out of my compound to hang with the cats. Now, cats are cool but they have some very odd habits. To begin with they have this nasty habit of eating things that are not food or even remotely edible. They eat plastic plants, rags and random pieces of garbage. Then they throw it up in a grotesque pile of vile fluid. And in a final act of madness, they go smell it as if it is some great achievement.

They also do this odd thing where they howl at random times of the day and night. It seems to serve no purpose other than to annoy every living thing within range. It is hard to describe how awful it was. It usually woke up Barney and of course the rest of the house.

I once asked Sparks why they did it.

"We're just being cats. It's what we do."

They also seemed to take great joy in just knocking random things over. They would shove over vases of flowers, cups, push things off shelves and drag clothes around the house. There seemed to be no method to their madness.

And then there was the drinking from the toilet. Just because you can do something doesn't mean you should.

Easter was now just a few days away and the activity in the house was at a fever pitch. I could hear the parents going over plans for food and then there was the subject of Uncle Mel. He was clearly not coming to the party because of something he did last year.

It was not clear what he did but Aunt Grace, his wife, was still on the list. I was wondering what he could have done to get himself banned from the party. I am sure it was some silly human thing.

Animals do not have many of the same silly and petty problems that humans do. First of all, we don't talk about politics, religion or other such things. In the animal world if you don't like someone you simply eat them or they eat you.

And little ones listen to their parents and elders or they get a claw, a paw or a hoof to the head. There are no debates, no excuses. You do as you are told and you are told once.

My father once said to me and my siblings, "There are two things I want to hear from you. Yes, sir and no, sir."

The parents then turned their attention to planning the menu for their big meal. There was going to be ham, turkey and fish. I did not hear any mention of rabbit which was a good thing. I was worried that since Easter seems to celebrate this giant bunny, rabbit might be on the menu. Fortunately, the only rabbit served would be the big giant chocolate candy kind.

The planning went on for what seemed like an hour as they counted chairs and plates and all the other things you need for a party. They then turned their attention to the baskets the children would receive on Easter morning.

They pulled three large baskets from a nearby closet that were filled with all sorts of candy, toys, books and other treats.

The baskets were filled with the greenest grass I have ever seen. I would later learn the hard way that it was not real. Yes, I had a cat moment. I am not proud.

I was rather surprised to see the baskets since I was led to believe the Easter Bunny brought the children gifts. It now seems it was the parents and it all felt like some big scam being played on the children. How awful it must be once they learned the truth.

I watched as the parents carefully placed the baskets in the living room. They left behind a small plate of food and three notes, one from each of the children.

After arranging it all neatly the father sat down and wrote three letters, one for each child. I just assumed they were supposed to be messages from the Easter Bunny to make the children believe it all.

The final touch was the mother, eating some of the food from the plate to make it look like the Easter Bunny had eaten some of the food. They missed no detail big or small. They must truly love their children to go through with such a grand ruse.

"Tomorrow is your big day," the father said pointing at me as he dumped some trash into the container nearby.

I was not sure what he meant by that. I was only hoping that it was a good thing. The mother came over and gave me a small pat on the head. They then turned out the lights in the kitchen and headed up to bed.

The lights in the house went out behind them as they walked up the stairs to the bedroom. I could hear Barney's nails scratch across the floor as he raced up the stairs to take up his position in the bedroom. Silence descended on the home.

I grabbed some food, a little drink of water and then settled in for the night. I did not sleep easy at first, wondering what the new day would bring.

An hour or two later I heard an odd noise coming from the living room. It didn't sound like the cats since I was familiar with the ways. This was something different. I jumped from my compound to go and investigate.

When I arrived in the front room, I found a glowing figure in the shape of a rabbit. I approached slowly, not sure what to make of what I was seeing.

"Hello, little one," the figure said. "How are you?"

"I am good, I think. Who are you?"

The figure laughed, "I am the Easter Bunny you have heard so much about."

"But..." I tried to say.

"But am I real?"

"Well yes. I was led to believe that you were a fantasy, a mythical creature created for children. I was told you are not real."

"Well, what do you think?"

"You certainly seem real. I mean you are here talking to me. But how do I know I am not just having a dream?"

"You don't."

"I am wondering why you are here. The parents have already put out presents. There are baskets filled with candy, toys and all sorts of other goodies. They have even left some food and letters from the children."

"Those are not the kind of gifts I bring."

"So, if you aren't bringing candy and toys what are you bringing?"

I bring gifts you cannot see or touch. I bring hope, peace, dreams, love and comfort."

"How can you give gifts you cannot see or touch?"

"To a child who lives in a world of violence and fear I bring them peace and healing. To the child who feels neglected and alone, I offer comfort and hope. To the child who feels lost I show them the path through the darkness. To the child who dreams of becoming an astronaut, a doctor, a scientist or more I give them inspiration to do the hard work ahead."

"How?"

"The greatest gifts are the ones you cannot buy, cannot make, cannot trade. They are the things that make you grow; help you live your best life. They are the things that help you know right from wrong, kindness from evil, teach you that bad things happen when good men and women turn away from the forces of darkness."

"It is the gift that allows you to see your mother and those who have come before you. How is it possible for you to still see her, still talk to her, still feel her presence?"

"I don't know. She just comes to me whenever I need her."

"And that has been one of my gift to you. The gift of vision to see what cannot be seen."

"Do you do this for everyone?"

"They are offered to all God's creatures big and small. But not all can accept them, see their value."

"So, you are real?"

"I am as real as your faith and hope allow. And now I must go."

"But I have so many questions."

"And you will have many days to find the answers. I can only tell you to remember not all gifts come in physical form and cannot be easily seen."

"Always look for the good in the world. Even in the darkest moments, it is always there. "

"Do you have a gift for me?"

"Yes, you will get it tomorrow. Just like everyone else. Patience. Goodbye."

"Goodbye and thanks. Will I see you again?"

"Perhaps. I don't make the rules."

And with that the light began to fade and then it was gone. I could not be sure what I had just experienced. Was I having a dream, some kind of odd reaction to something I ate or was it all indeed real?

Easter morning came and the children raced down the stairs. They immediately focused on the gifts like a bee to honey. Tearing them open to get to the goodies inside.

There was nothing unusual about it all until I spotted Max, the oldest child pulling a book from his basket about astronomy. I had heard him talk about how he one day wanted to travel into space and explore the stars.

Yet this was no ordinary gift, this was a gift that brought light to this small child. It was a gift of inspiration. It was a gift he could not see, could not touch but it was a gift that would help lead him down the path he had chosen.

The book was very real and something he could touch. His mother and father smiled; unaware the book contained the real gift, the one they could not see. Years later Max would find the book and be reminded how his love of space was ignited on that Easter Sunday when he had received it.

As I turned to begin eating my breakfast, I spotted a tiny Gerber Daisy hidden in the back of my cage. My mom and I would often sit in fields of daisies as she taught me about the world around us. I closed my eyes and held the flower against my chest. Her image and presence came flooding over me.

It was only then that I realized just how lonely I had been feeling, how cut off from the real world. It was my gift. I could see us sitting in the sun in the fields of home. It felt so real.

"You may think you are alone," her voice whispered. "but I am always with you. Always."

Before I could think another thought I was rudely yanked from my cage. The guests for the party were starting to arrive and I was to be one of the star attractions. I was passed around the room like an appetizer tray fearful someone was going to drop me.

I was squeezed, kissed, hugged and bombarded with an annoying array of animal baby talk. Everyone wanted to get a picture with me. I was getting my 15 minutes of fame. It all ended when dinner was announced and I was suddenly dropped to the floor and left unattended.

I hopped slowly over to join the cats who were sitting in a straight line taking in the show.

"Hey," Snowflake said.

"Hey, guys. How long do you think it's gonna take before someone notices that I am running free?"

"Hours," Kingdom replied. "If you think Barney eats like an animal wait until you see this group chow down. It's like watching a race to the fat man buffet. I think you are the least of their concerns right now."

Kingdom was right. The feast went on for over an hour with food flying everywhere. And there were the three cats and Barney scooping it up as pieces fell to the floor.

I sat and took it all in. I had no interest in eating most of what was falling in front of me. I was more concerned that

Barney and the cats would explode from all the food they were eating.

"How was it?" I asked as Snowflake walked past me, his stomach scraping along the ground.

"Outstanding. Four paws up," he joked.

We all watched from a distance as dessert was served.

"Anyone want to tell me what Uncle Mel did to get banned?" I asked to break the silence.

The three cats looked at each other mentally debating whether to answer the question.

"Let's just say some things cannot be unseen, some things cannot be taken back once said," Sparks said.

"If you hang around humans long enough you are going to see them do some awfully stupid things. Think of the worst thing you have ever seen a human do, multiple it by 10 and that's Uncle Mel."

We sat and watched in silence as the dinner slowly started to wind down. There were toasts, photos to mark the occasion and promises of future gatherings that would never happen.

When Aunt Grace announced her plans to leave it gave everyone an excuse to make a rush for the exits. She had learned that telling everyone it was not great for an old woman to drive alone in the dark was a great way to make a graceful exit.

Leftovers were given to anyone they could be forced on. The rest would end up as leftovers or be dumped in the trash. Humans seemed to have no concept of what true hunger was like, how difficult it was to find that next meal in the wild and why animals never let anything go to waste. There were no Walmarts where animals could go shopping.

The party officially ended when the last guests were safely escorted out the door. The parents collapsed in a heap of relief and the kids went back to playing their video games.

"I think that went rather well," the mother said.

"Yes," the father confirmed. "Everyone seemed to like the food, there were no awkward moments and no trouble like last year."

And with that, they both looked down and spotted me sitting on the floor. I was looking right at them, sitting in a proper pose.

"What is Werner doing out?" they said in unison.

"I think we all just kinda forgot about him. Sarah, you want to put your little friend away. I am sure he had a busy time eating a lot of things he shouldn't have."

Sarah came up and gently scooped me up off the ground. She gave me a kiss on the head and a big hug before carrying me back to my compound. She made me a plate of food and dropped it into my cage. I was lucky to get that. She walked off before giving me any pellets, hay or fresh water.

Everyone in the family was now in clean-up mode. I was an afterthought. I was now starting to understand why cats drank from toilets.

The tables were cleared, the dishwasher jammed to capacity and yet there was still a pile of dishes several feet high. There were still several hours of work ahead.

"Let's just finish in the morning dear," the father finally said. "This is a bigger job than I can deal with right now."

Mom nodded in agreement and they did a last look around and ordered the kids to bed. The kids ran up the stairs with their Easter bounty in hand. The mother, father and Barney soon followed, the lights going out as they advanced toward their bedroom.

The upstairs bedroom light was the last to be extinguished and the door closed. The home once again fell silent. This day was over.

EASTER HANGOVER

In the days after Easter, I seemed to become invisible to the world. The pets and hugs I used to get were now gone. No one came by to play with me and there were even times when they forgot to feed me.

The neglect also led to a growing problem with the litter box. I was now lucky if someone came around once a week to change it. It soon became a source of serious tension in the household.

"Sarah," her father called out. "I thought you promised to take care of this little guy. Look at his area. It's a mess."

"But Dad, I've been busy," Sarah excused.

"Well, he has no food, his water dish is empty and this litter box is atrocious. You don't even feed him half the time. That's mean. How would you like it if I didn't feed you? Either clean this up and start taking care of him or he has to go."

Wait, going where I thought. I kinda just got here. I am not crazy about getting dumped somewhere else.

"Yes, dad," Sarah said with her head down. She started to clean up my compound but I could tell her heart was not in it. I felt bad because I had tried to do the best I could to keep it clean. But I am a rabbit and don't have any hands to clean anything but myself. If they let me outside, I could actually feed myself and find water.

The scene would be repeated over and over in the days and weeks ahead. Mom and dad would yell, Sarah would clean things up and we would start all over again. Sarah may not have realized or cared but I knew I was on thin ice and time was running out. I thought more and more about trying to escape back to the outside world.

The end came suddenly one night when her mother came home from work and found my compound in disarray once again.

"Sarah," she screamed.

Sarah came running down the stairs.

"That's it. This rabbit has to go. You are not taking care of him. Look how skinny he is from not eating. And the smell and mess from his cage is out of control."

"But mom, I will do better. Give me another chance."

"You are out of chances young lady. You made a promise and you did not keep it."

"What's going on in here?" the father said coming in to check on the source of the racket that had the whole house up in arms.

"I want this rabbit out of here. Put it in the garage, take it back to the pet shop or just give it to someone who wants to take care of it. I am done with this."

"But it's not his fault," the father argued in my defense. "He's just an innocent little animal."

"Innocent or not he has to go. We can find a new home for him."

"Dad," Sarah pleaded.

"Sorry honey, you had more than enough chances. This is the best thing for everyone."

I could see Sarah start to cry as the father picked me up and shoved me into a cage. Her tears were too late to save me. He packed the cage with food, water and hay and then took me out to the garage.

And just like that, I was left in a cage, on a workbench in a cold dark garage. There were spiders and all manner of creepy things about. I had to shoo mice away from my food dish almost every night. I guess they were hungry too.

The only light came in through a small two-pane window during the day. The sun never quite reached my cage. I tried to stretch to reach its warmth but it was just out of range.

I was now a prisoner. Once a day someone would come out and toss some lettuce in my cage and fill my water bottle. I didn't eat my hay on some nights so I could use it to stay warm. My cage was suspended over a hole in the bench which was a bit unnerving at first. I kept feeling like I was going to fall through to the ground. My feet were getting sores from walking across the metal grating on the bottom of the cage. Bunnies are meant to walk on grass, not metal cages.

I was left hanging in space because there was no litter box now and anytime, I had to go it dropped through the floor of the cage into a box below. It was much more efficient for my human captors. Not so good for me. The smell was awful since no one ever came to change it.

Each time the family started up a car to head off to work, to school, to a night out or any other event the garage filled with toxic fumes. If the conditions in the cage didn't kill me, the fumes soon would. It seemed like the world had abandoned me.

One night I was lying in the cage when the light of the moon bathed my cage in a brilliant white light. I could sense my mom was with me telling me not to give up, not to lose hope. It was so hard, so cold. I was so hungry, so very alone.

The father was now the only one who came to feed me and offer any kind words. I thought about trying to escape when he opened the door but wasn't sure if I would survive the winter which was raging outside.

One night the mother and father came back from a night out and the headlights happened to shine on my cage as they pulled in. I was now dirty and cold. I could see my shadow shiver because I had lost the fat I needed to stay warm. I was a pathetic sight.

"We really need to do something with him," the father said. "It is kind of cruel to leave him out here. Look at him. When is the last time someone let him out of that thing?"

"Well, he's not coming back in the house. Can't you find someone to take him?"

"The pet shop won't take him back and I checked with all of our family and friends. No one wants a rabbit. It's not your everyday kind of pet. I even called the zoo."

"Well, maybe you can just let him go."

"You mean dump him out into the winter? There is a foot of snow on the ground and it's gonna be near zero tonight."

"Well, he has fur and he is a wild animal. He will be okay. We can throw some food out for him. It's better than leaving him in here."

The father looked at me and then back at his wife.

"Okay, let me sleep on it. I am surely not going to release him in the middle of the night. What will I tell Sarah"?

"Just tell her we found him a new home. I doubt she will even know he is gone."

The next morning the father came in and picked up my cage. He took me to a wooded area several miles from the family home. He walked around to the back of the car, opened the door and pulled out my cage.

"Sorry guy. We don't have a choice. This will be good for you. You are going back to nature where you belong."

Really, I thought. Back to nature in the middle of winter.

He opened the cage but I refused to get out. He tried to lure me out with some carrots and apples but I was not that stupid. He finally just dumped the cage and sent me crashing into the snow that covered the ground.

I stood there in shock. I turned to the father and raised up on my hind legs to ask for mercy. I could see tears welling up in his eyes as he tried to wave me away. I walked up to him and tried to grab the legs of his pants with my paws but he simply bent down and gave me a final pat on the head.

"Good luck little guy. You are going to be okay. I am sure you will find plenty of friends out here."

And with that, he stood up, tossed some food into the snow, walked back to his car, got in and drove off. There was little time for a pity party since he had dumped me in the middle of an open field and I was great prey for the many animals in the forest desperate for a winter meal. Food does not come easy for anyone in winter.

Being white would be an advantage as long as the snow remained on the ground. I would blend in easily and digging a temporary den to keep warm and seek shelter would be much easier. Finding food would be a much more difficult task. I ate what I could from what had been left behind and carried what I could.

Night fell and I was quickly reminded that the world was a scary and dangerous place. It was cold, so very cold and I was so very hungry. My first goal would be to survive the night.

There would be no sleep. My wild senses quickly turned back on. In the wilderness, every noise, scent, movement can mean danger to a rabbit. Back in my human home, I had learned to ignore the sounds. They were all part of a mechanical rhythm that was no threat. Here, everything was a threat.

It was cold outside but the snow on the ground provided a nice place for me to create a warm burrow. I was safe from the cold and the snow would provide a source of water until morning.

Things were nice and peaceful until just before dawn when I sensed something was wrong. The sound was faint at first but then slowly began to build. Something was heading my way. It could be any number of things, most of them bad.

I slowly gathered my feet beneath me, ready to launch into action. I moved slowly so as not to draw attention to my position.

As each moment passed it became more and more clear something had picked up on my scent. I could feel my heart beginning to race. And then the world fell silent.

It was now a standoff, prey against predator. Each of us was waiting for the other to make the first move. I slowly deployed my ears and began to pick up the heartbeat and breathing of my new enemy.

It was coming from directly behind me. It was also now well within striking distance.

And then I heard the creature take a deep breath and push off to strike. Before I could get airborne, I could feel a set of sharp teeth sink into my back right leg.

The creature began to throw me around hoping to disorient me and deliver a crippling blow. I could see the snow around me starting to turn red. The bite had struck home.

I was not going to surrender quietly. I used my front and back paws to slash across the face of my foe. I could hear a yelp letting me know that my attack had inflicted some damage.

The creature jumped on top of me and I struck again tearing across its belly, ripping it open. It was enough to stun him and give me the chance to escape.

As I ran off, I could see a coyote in full pursuit. It was going to take some skill and luck to get away. He had the advantage of knowing the terrain and habitat.

As the chase began to play out, I could sense the injuries I had inflicted on the coyote were causing him some distress. He was slow to respond each time I turned in a different direction. He was obviously struggling to make moves to the left or right.

I could once again feel his hot breath on my back as we raced along the floor of the forest. He made another lunge at me but the attack was blocked by some thick brush.

I decided to circle him and take advantage of his injuries. We ran back over an area we had already covered and I could see a large amount of blood in the snow.

After a minute or two it was over. When I was convinced that it was safe, I started to slow down to find a place to attend to my wounds.

I came upon a stream that still had some open water. There was plenty of thicket around the area to conceal my presence.

When I finally got a chance to check my wounds, I discovered they were deeper than I had thought. I was able to stop the bleeding by packing snow over it. The snow also helped to ease the pain.

The area where I was now sitting seemed to be safe though there was a large trail of blood leading to my location. It would not be hard for the coyote or some other predator to find me. After I had stopped the bleeding, I moved upstream a bit to help cover my scent.

I came across a hollowed-out tree that looked like a good spot to seek shelter. It looked empty and was nice and deep to keep larger animals out. I was lucky enough to find some dead leaves to eat. It wasn't much but it was better than nothing.

I would stay hidden there for several days feeling better and better as each new day arrived. Winter was slowly starting to surrender its grip on the world. The snow was melting and I could start to see the first patches of bare ground. It would still be weeks before any real amount of vegetation would break through the ground.

The need for food was now becoming more and more desperate. I had lost a lot of weight and was starting to feel a little dizzy. Foraging for food in my condition was becoming a serious issue.

It was now becoming clear that I was going to have to venture out from the safe home I had made if I was going to survive. There was nothing nearby for me to eat.

I made my way into a large field where I spotted a flock of birds around a large feeder. It was a menagerie of the aviation world. There were cardinals, sparrows, blue jays and even a couple of ducks. There was a house on the top that no respectable bird would live in.

There were a lot of seeds falling to the ground as the birds above fought for food, dropping more than they ate. Below was a small zoo of squirrels, rabbits, raccoons and others feasting on the food as it fell.

I approached with caution, ears up, nose and whiskers at work, trying to detect any sign of trouble. I nibbled a few seeds on the outer rings of the feast as I moved closer and closer to the large pile a few feet in front of me.

Everyone was in a sharing mood since there was plenty to eat. I had been eating for only a few seconds when a loud blast shattered the quiet of the morning like breaking glass.

A squirrel just a few feet away fell in a heap to the ground. I could see the light had gone out in his eyes as another gunshot went off. The second shot took down a rabbit. He struggled to stand and crawled a few feet before going down for good.

Someone was using the seed to lure in animals and hunt them down. I guess everyone has to eat. It is nature's way.

I grabbed what I could and immediately took off for the safety of the woods. I heard several more shots behind me as I ran. I did not know how many others were hit and was not going to slow down to look.

I made it back to my shelter along the stream just as a massive spring storm started to roll in. The violent transition from winter to spring brought lightning, vicious thunder and torrential rain. It was followed by a monstrous wind. The trees in the forest had to fight valiantly not only to keep their branches but to keep their roots from being ripped right out of the ground. It took everything they had to hold on.

The area that was once safe was now starting to flood and I had no choice but to venture out into the storm to keep from drowning. Hungry, tired and afraid I set out to find new shelter. I saw plenty of animals out doing the same. It was a mass migration from the forest to any place safe.

Every time I thought I had found a spot I would find someone else had beaten me to it. I once again came upon the yard with the big feeder in it, but did not dare enter.

After a few minutes, I stumbled into an area with several homes side by side. However, many of them had dogs. Never a safe place to be. There were also signs of coyotes and foxes in the area. There was also the threat from above. The storm had forced several hawks and owls from their homes.

Just when I thought the situation was hopeless, I came across a large yard with a garden and a small pond in it. Nothing had been planted yet and harvest would be months away but there were plenty of places to hide.

I was exhausted, starving and now infested with ticks trying to make a meal of me. A crawled up under a small bridge that was in the garden. It would provide good shelter from enemies on the ground and from above. Before I could think about looking for food or water, I was asleep.

That sleep was interrupted a few hours later with a large bang. A rather old-looking man had emerged from the house to toss out the evening trash. The slamming of the garbage can lid had startled me. My movement gave away my position.

I tried not to move as the old man approached with a stick and a flashlight in hand.

"Harold, what are you doing?" his wife called out.

"There's something out here," he replied.

"What is it? If it's another raccoon I'll bring the bat. I am tired of them eating the garbage and making a mess."

"No. It's something else. I think it's a rabbit."

"Be careful. They have rabies. Just leave it be. I will call the police."

It turned into a standoff, the man staring at me and me staring right back. I must have passed out again because the next thing I remember were blue lights flashing everywhere.

"Hey there small one. How are you doing?" a gentle new voice called from the darkness.

I tried to stand and run off but it was just a struggle to move at this point. I was cornered, exhausted and at the mercy of whatever was standing in the darkness in front of me.

Just when I thought all was lost a carrot emerged from the darkness. I had to weigh the potential danger of taking it against the powerful feeling of hunger that had taken over my body.

"Come on. It's okay. We are here to help."

Hunger can make you do crazy and desperate things so I emerged from my hiding spot and walked toward the voice offering me the carrot.

The voice belonged to a large policeman. I took the carrot and he gently picked me up. I felt that I would be safe, at least for the time being.

"He's so cute," the man's female partner said. "How did you get out here little fellow?"

"Unit 12 to base," the male officer called.

"Go ahead."

"We have an animal in custody here. Turns out the intruder is not a burglar or mass killer but a small white rabbit. It came running right up to me. I am pretty sure this is someone's pet. It is clearly not a wild animal from the looks of it. It either escaped or got dumped out into the street. It's pure white with red eyes and is in pretty sad shape."

"Okay, send in a photo and we will post it on social media to see if we get any hits on him. From the sound of this, I am guessing this is a bunny given as an Easter gift that someone doesn't want anymore."

"Take him over to Dr. Phillips. He handles the strays and abandoned animals."

"Copy that."

With that, the two officers took me inside their car and we drove off. I licked their hands as we went along, trying to show my appreciation. I wasn't sure where I was going but it had to be a lot better than where I had been.

"What do we have here?" a nice young woman in an all-green lab outfit asked. I was now in a tiny room, sitting on a table.

"We have a rabbit," one of the officers offered. "We found him over on 9th and Willow. He came right up to me and has been licking my hand. He seems to be a pretty gentle dude. He was our easiest call of the night."

"But he does not appear to be in very good shape," the woman said, "He is scared skinny, dirty and full of bugs. Let's take a closer look."

She did the usual inspection, prying open my mouth to check my teeth. She then squeezed and prodded the rest of my parts. I was pretty sure I was all still there. She then tossed me on a scale.

"Yikes, just a little over four pounds. That's not good. Did you post him on Missing Pets yet?"

"Yes, but I have a feeling we won't hear anything on this one. This looks like the classic Easter bunny dump."

"Well, we will do what we can for him. He has seven days. Let's hope someone shows up to claim him."

Fat chance I thought to myself. I doubt the people who dumped me out in to the cold were going to come looking for me and then take me back.

"Why does he only have 7 days?" one of the officers asked.

"All the strays have 7 days. The state pays us to take care of them for a week in the theory someone might come to claim them. Most of the time they don't and we have to put them down."

"That seems pretty cruel."

"If we don't do it this way we would be overrun with strays and we just don't have the budget to take care of all the animals people dump."

"Why would someone dump a cute little guy like this out into the cold?"

"Because humans can sometimes be jerks. They don't realize the responsibility they have when they take a pet in. They are everything to that animal. They are the ones that pet has to look to for food, shelter, medicine if they get sick and for love."

"I will start the clock on this guy tomorrow morning since it's so late in the day. That gives him until next Friday. Thanks for bringing him in. At least he gets a chance, so many others of these abandoned and lost pets don't. Very bad things happen to them. They starve, get hit by cars or fall prey to larger predators."

"Stay safe," the woman said as the two officers turned to leave.

"You too," they said in unison.

After the officers left, I was stuffed into a cage. I say stuffed because it was very small, leaving me with barely enough room to turn around.

There was one of those annoying pet bottles, a small bowl of pellets and some hay. That was it. I got the feeling that I was not going to be here for very long. I was not sure if that was good or bad. But it was warm, I had food and was safe.

The accommodations were spartan, to say the least. There were two cats and a small dog in the other five cages in the room. They were all the same size so I was wondering what they did to any larger animals that came in. Maybe I didn't want to know.

The days quickly went by. Friday turned into Saturday, then Sunday. I knew what the woman meant by put down. Since I knew no one was coming for me my only real option was to escape.

It would not be easy. The cages were not only air-tight; they were ten feet off the floor. It would not be easy or wise to attempt a jump from that height. Bad things happen when bunnies slam into floors from high places.

Each morning when they opened my cage to feed me and change the water, I looked for a way to escape. One of the cats, who were equally desperate, jumped into the arms of one of the attendants begging for mercy. There would be none.

Later that day the cat was taken from the room. It did not come back. The second cat disappeared the day after that leaving just me and a small dog named Biscuit.

His story would have a happy ending. In the middle of the afternoon on his fourth day, a little boy came running in and grabbed him from his cage. Biscuit had run away for some reason. The silly fellow had decided that he did not like the pampered life of a house pet, fed, cared for and love by that little boy. He had spent a few days on the streets before being found by the same two officers who found me.

It appeared that he had learned his lesson, jumping into the boy's arms, licking his face and showing how sorry and stupid he felt for running off. I am guessing he would not do it again.

That left me all alone, sitting in a cage, waiting for no one, the clock ticking. I started to feel lonely and sad. When I could sleep, I have dreams of my days in the fields. When I was awake, I wondered if it was going to hurt when they ended me. I truly hoped that it would not hurt.

I wondered how many innocent pets meet their end this way. Tossed away just because some human found them a chore, an inconvenience, a life not worth living.

I was napping when the doors to the room popped open.

"Hey Jan. How was your vacation?" the woman who had been caring for me asked the new person entering the room.

"It was nice. What's the deal with this one?" she asked in a no-nonsense tone.

"He goes down tomorrow. He has been here since last Thursday night. I delayed the intake to give him an extra day to make sure you were here. There have been no inquiries. He's a lost little boy no one seems to want."

"We'll see about that," Jan said in a defiant tone.

"You can't save them all," the young girl said.

"Well, I am going to save this one."

And with that Jan picked up the phone and started making phone calls. I could tell things were not going well by the tone in her voice and the look on her face as she hung up after each call.

"Well, you are my last hope. You have 8 hours to help save this bunny. Do whatever you can, twist some arms, tug at some heartstrings. I know that no one likes to adopt these Florida whites but he is super cute and super smart. We have until 5 PM when we close. "

Jan took a break from her sales pitch to let the person on the other end of the phone speak.

"Okay, call me one way or the other."

The next few hours of my life flew by and dragged on, waiting for that phone to ring. Waiting for someone to say yes. An hour before closing time the phone rang.

"Yes," Jan listened with no emotion on her face. And then the words I wanted to hear.

"Excellent. She needs to get here by 5 PM. I will have him ready. 5 PM. No later. What's her name?"

There was more silence as Jan started to write something down on a pad of paper.

"Okay, Sharon Miller. She will foster? Okay, not the perfect situation, adoption is better. But we need to get this little guy out of here before Dr. Death does his thing. It's not right to take these animals in, take the money and then put them to sleep."

The person on the other end said something that I couldn't hear.

"Okay, thanks again. 5 PM."

As soon as she got off the phone, she turned into a human tornado putting together a care package of food, toys, medicine and a long list of other items.

She then picked me up and gave me a kiss saying," You be a good boy now. I don't want to see you back here."

Four o'clock turned into 4:15 and then 4:30. Time was running out and there was still no sign of this Sharon person.

Maybe she had gotten lost, in a car crash or worse yet, maybe she had changed her mind.

Whatever the case, she was my only hope and time was running out. The doors close at 5 PM, and under state law so do the books on me. The doors to the facility would be locked and, in the morning, I would be toast.

But Sharon would not fail me. 15 minutes before the deadline she came crashing through the front door.

"I'm here," she announced in a frantic voice. "I am here for the bunny."

"Excellent," Jan said. "I was getting a little worried.

"Sorry, I am so late. I kinda got hung up in traffic. It took longer to get here than I thought."

"No worries. You are here now to save the day."

"What can you tell me about him?"

"He is a male, maybe a year old. He is seriously underweight but doesn't have any serious health issues from what I can see."

"Does he have a name?"

"Believe it or not I found some writing behind his right ear. Looks like someone wrote Werner with a magic marker."

"Werner?"

"That's odd."

"Yes. It looks like a child may have written it. If I had to bet, I would guess mom or dad thought it would be a great present for Easter. The child was too young to understand the difference between a real rabbit and a toy one so she wrote the name on it. I am gonna say the bunny was named after a family member or a cartoon character from some TV show. Who knows?"

"I am going to guess the child didn't take care of the rabbit and mom and dad decided it had to go. So, they thought it would be a great idea to just release it into the wild. They might have even believed they were doing the rabbit a favor. Wild rabbit, domestic rabbit, it's all the same to them."

"Wow."

"So, I have everything here you need. There is a cage, food, some medications he may need and the papers you have to sign."

"Can I pick him up?"

"Of course."

I knew I was safe as soon as Sharon picked me up and gave me a gentle kiss on the head. I was home.

"Poor little thing. I am going to take great care of you. I promise."

Sharon talked to me the entire way home, telling me all about the bunnies she had taken care of in the past. And she told me about all of the cool things she had waiting for me back at her house. It sounded pretty good.

When we walked into her home I was greeted by this giant bear of a man. His name was Roy. He had an odd name, just like me.

Sharon showed me around the house. There would be plenty of room to run in this place. The compound she had set up with filled with all sorts of toys, food and fun stuff to do.

She carried me into the kitchen where they started to give me a thorough inspection. Roy started to pull the ticks from my fur.

"Sharon," he said. "He is so skinny. I can feel his bones. There is no meat on him. We need to fatten him up."

"Well, he has come to the right place. Just remember this is a rabbit, not a dog. That means no pizza, ice cream, candy or other garbage. He eats lettuce, hay and pellets."

" Well, he's not going to gain weight eating that crap," Roy laughed.

"Bunnies need a healthy diet not to feed out of the garbage."

"Maybe just a little here and there?"

"No junk food. Period," Sharon barked.

"Oh, Good grief Charlie Brown," Roy cried out. "He is covered with ticks. They are everywhere. We need to get them off."

For the next 20 minutes, they pulled tick after tick from my fur. Sharon also took some time to cut my nails which were now so long it was becoming tough to walk on flat indoor surfaces. They washed the worst of the mud off my fur and tried to do their best to clean me up.

I could tell from her touch that Sharon had cared for bunnies before. Roy seemed clueless about the care and treatment of my species. I found it rather amusing that he was afraid to pick me up for fear he might drop me. I was a bunny, not a human baby.

After doing their best to clean me up Sharon placed me down in my new compound. The food I found inside was a buffet beyond my wildest dreams. There were four different kinds of lettuce. There were pellets, water and even a few treats.

I was shameless in the way I attacked the pile of food before me. I could feel my belly start to fill and drag on the ground. It was good to have some real food in my body for the first time in weeks

After eating I went on a tour of my new home. In addition to the food, there was a water bowl, a major upgrade from the bottle I had endured at the vet's office. There were toys and sticks and all sorts of things to keep me entertained. There was even a bunny blanket in the pen so I could cuddle up on something soft at night. It felt like bunny heaven.

THE HOUSE OF SHARON

The House of Sharon was a grand place except for a few of the rules. 1-Don't eat any wires. Now, that's a tough rule because bunnies love to chew things. It's good for our teeth. Wires are a special treat because they are just so much fun. Humans can't hear the buzzing but we can.

Rule number 2, don't eat anything else that isn't your food, isn't given to you to play with or offered up as a treat to perform a shameless trick. That would include shoes, hats, rugs, books, furniture, remote control devices, plants or pretty much anything else. This of course conflicts with bunny law which states anything left out can and should be chewed or eaten.

Rule 3 was an easy one and one that I agreed with, keep the poop in the litter box. Bunnies are very clean by their nature. If you watch them closely for any length of time you will see they are always cleaning themselves. And no one likes running around in their own poop. We are not common pet rabble after all.

Other than that, there were no real rules. I could roam around pretty much anywhere I wanted except for a few rooms with lots of wires that were blocked off. I was a free-range chicken.

It was easy to tell when I did something wrong because Sharon would yell out "Werner J." I wasn't sure what the J meant but she would always add it to the end of my name and it always meant trouble.

Roy on the other hand would pretty much let me do whatever I wanted. He was very much a creature of habit like me. He liked to do the same things, at the same time each day.

Each morning Roy and Sharon would get up. One of them would feed me. Roy would always give me more to eat than Sharon. He would give me three carrots instead of two, four different kinds of veggies instead of one or two. And the bowl of pellets would weigh just a little bit more. It was just his way.

After they fed me, Sharon would go off and have her toast and coffee. Roy would feast on an apple, a banana and Cheerios. Now, the Cheerios were right from the box, no milk, no bowl, just dip your hand in the box and grab a handful feeding. Sharon found it barbaric. But only humans use utensils. There is nothing wrong with eating right out of a box or bag.

I quickly learned that if I stood up on my hind legs and begged Roy would share a little of his breakfast with me. I would get two or three bites of his banana, a bite from the apple and two Cheerios. It was the same amount in the same order every day. It would never vary. Ever. That was unless he was having his second most favorite breakfast, little chocolate donuts and orange juice. I would never get any of that.

The orange juice I didn't really care about. Oranges were okay but not my thing. Now, those chocolate donuts, that was another story. Sharon had made it clear bunnies did not eat chocolate donuts. I beg to differ.

Now, Roy wouldn't give me a donut but I would enjoy the crumbs. When Roy ate, there were always crumbs. I could see why he liked them and longed for the day he would offer one up. It would never happen. Crumbs would have to do.

I spent most of my day napping and wandering around the house. If Roy and Sharon went out, I would sneak into the rooms in the house where I had been banned. I loved the bathroom, especially on hot days where I could lay on the cool tile. I often got caught in there because it was such an awesome place to sleep.

The day would roll along and soon it would be dinner for humans. They got to eat whenever they wanted. I was restricted to two meals a day. It didn't seem fair.

However, there were always crumbs. There were tiny pieces of bread, vegetables, meat and an assortment of things I had never tasted before. After dinner, the real treat would come, pretzels. If they were home Roy would sometimes settle in for some TV with a bag of pretzels at his side.

Good golly Miss Molly did I love pretzels. I was hooked the first time I had one.

Now, Sharon would monitor my treat intake closely and I was only allowed one stick pretzel a night. It was just not right.

Roy knew that when he pulled out the pretzels, I would not be far behind. He would try to hide them from me by muffling the sound of the bag, stashing them in a towel or putting them in a plastic lunch bag that made less noise.

But these efforts were useless because bunnies don't really rely on sight or hearing when it comes to a snack. They rely on smell. And it was not hard to miss the smell of pretzels and other snacks when the scent was in the air.

I would jump up on the couch and do the cute bunny thing. Roy would scrape off the salt, thinking it would somehow protect me from high blood pressure. It would always result in a treat. Yet, no matter how much I begged I would only get a single pretzel. I blame Sharon.

Sharon was always trying to teach Roy the ways of the bunny. But it seemed a lost cause. She would go through the list of things that were good and bad for bunnies. Luckily Roy never seemed to listen to most of it.

Roy's treats were always better than Sharon's. Sharon would give me the healthy bunny treats from the pet store, chosen with great care. Roy would give me the stuff you won't find in the forest, pretzels, chips, cookies and more.

While Roy was taking care of my physical needs Sharon was trying to make sure I was getting the education I needed. She would buy all sorts of educational toys.

There were balls that I would roll around to get a treat. Sharon had this device where I had to slide a door open to get a treat. She even tried to get me to obey some basic commands. Now, she meant well and I loved the treats but sorry, I am no dog. I am a rabbit.

The highlight of each year would of course be Easter. Sharon had a pretty large collection of stuffed rabbits and she would place me in the middle of them for what she called the Easter Parade.

The first time it happened I must admit that I was a little freaked out. I was dropped down in the middle of a dozen or so stuffed toy rabbits, many of them looked very real. I wasn't sure what to make of it at first but soon got the idea that Sharon wanted a picture of me with the rest of the toys. It was her special way of celebrating Easter, in a bunny way.

As the years went by, I learned to look in the right direction so she could get the best shot to show her friends. I didn't mind. It was a strange custom but humans are strange creatures and making her feel good was a small price to pay for all the kindness she showed me every day.

My favorite time of year was the spring and summer when they would open the back door and I could listen to all of the sounds outside, take in all of the smells. I would nap in the sunshine feeling its embrace.

It was also the time of year when the Honey Locust tree in the backyard would bloom. Roy had learned from watching the wild rabbits roaming the yard that rabbits loved the leaves from the tree. He also learned that rabbits loved the White Clover many humans saw as weeds. To rabbits, they were juicy taste treats.

Roy was good that way. He would often feed me things that he saw the wild rabbits eating, figuring I would like them too. He was right. He might not have looked like the brightest star in the universe but I give him credit for trying.

At night if Sharon and Roy were home they would watch TV. I found this activity most unusual. They would sit before a screen displaying many of the same things they could see if they simply turned around and looked out the window.

I tried to watch from time to time but found most of the shows rather silly. There were shows about people simply yelling at each other. There were shows about people fixing houses and taking great trips. There seemed to be a lot of shows about these things called zombies. I didn't like zombie movies especially the ones with zombie animals.

There were also a lot of shows about people traveling in space. I thought I would quite like traveling in space to see all of the amazing things there. I hoped that I would be around to see the first bunny head into space.

The funniest thing would always be watching them when sporting events were on. One week their team would win and they would be dancing for joy and very happy. The next week their team would lose and they would throw things at the TV and use all sorts of language there is no bunny translation for.

My favorite shows were the ones about nature. I liked learning about my place in the universe and how things came to be in the natural world. I did not like the shows where they showed animals eating other animals.

From time to time there would be holidays where family and friends came over. It was a grand time for me because it was a whole new set of humans to meet. Most of them would of course want to pick me up and give me pets, hugs and treats.

I especially loved the small humans because they were small like me. Sharon often gave the children little treats to feed me which brought giant smiles to their faces. It made me feel good to bring such joy to the world. I could often feel my mother's presence at moments like this.

I am not sure how the petting table began but I know that it was awesome. I loved to climb, something you would not expect from a rabbit. I would jump up on the table near where Sharon sat and she would pet me. It was very nice for me and for her.

I was also very lucky in that I was able to spend summertime in the city and winter in the country.

During the summertime, I would sit at the back door feeling the breeze come floating. I could listen to the sounds beyond the screen that protected me from the outside world.

Of course, Roy was always there to serve as my personal bodyguard should anything truly dangerous come around.

On cooler days I would climb up into the window and bask in the warm rays of the sun. As fall approached and the world grew cooler, they would light the fireplace. I would sit next to it for hours, staring at the flames and enjoying the warmth.

When autumn arrived, the leaves began to fall. From time to time, one would float into the house and I would enjoy a special taste treat. The leaves would come in many different colors. They would eventually cover everything and the trees outside my window would stand bare, ready for the winter to come.

The first notice of winter would arrive when snowflakes would parachute down from the sky. It was then Sharon and Roy would pack up the car to begin the journey to Florida. It would be my first trip to this amazing land of sun and warmth.

I was packed into a cage in the back seat of the car. The cage was filled with all sorts of treats to keep me occupied. I felt like a human teenager, given every convenience to guarantee compliance and silence on the road trip ahead.

I slept and ate most of the time as we traveled along the road. From time to time, I would catch a glimpse of the landscape as we passed by. The world outside my window would slowly transform from snow-covered fields and barren trees to the first signs of green on the ground and tiny buds on the trees.

When the door would open as we stopped for gas the air streaming in would grow warmer and warmer with each stop. It was a sign that we were growing closer and closer to our destination with each mile. The coats and hats Sharon and Roy wore at the beginning of the trip gave way to t-shirts and shorts.

I was amazed at how big America is. It seemed to go on and on. There were mountains, rivers, forests, farm fields and cities. It was green and blue, yellow and gray and all shades of the rainbow. What a grand creation it was.

My favorite time of day would come when we pull over for the night at a motel to take a break. Not many bunnies get to take a road trip or stay in a motel. So, I felt very special.

At night when Sharon and Roy would fall asleep, I would have full run of the room. I got to climb couches, scoot under beds and chairs. One of the great joys would be jumping up the bed. It was nice and soft.

Of course, I could not resist the temptation to jump on Roy and Sharon. Sharon would usually sleep through most of it. I loved to jump on Roy's head to roust him from a sound sleep. He would shriek like a little girl mouse. I would scurry off into the darkness before he could figure out what had happened. After three or four incidents he would finally figure out it was me and place a pillow over his head.

Arriving in Florida would always be quite a shock. Everything was green and there were a lot more sounds in the air. The smells were also much different since we were not far from the ocean.

Florida was a very cool place because we lived on the second floor and it had a lanai where I could look out at the animal kingdom below. By day the birds ruled the skies. They always seemed to be singing and looking for their next meal.

At night the real predators would come out. They were the things with legs and big teeth. Things that could run fast and make a quick meal of a small creature like me. I felt safe on my second-floor perch.

During the day there were always a lot of humans wandering down below. They would walk along the river that was not far from us. Others would sit and just look out enjoying the view.

I would amuse myself by watching their reactions when they first spotted me. Most humans thought I was a statue at first. From time to time, I would move just enough to get them questioning whether I was alive or fake.

I would try to catch the eye of one person sitting at the nearby pool and begin my game with a tiny movement.

"Did that thing just move?" a man would say to his wife pointing my way.

She would turn around and I would remain motionless.

"Dear, you are losing your mind," she would say turning back toward the book she had been enjoying.

Just as she turned away, I would hop two or three feet to the left or right. The man, seeing my movement, would once again motion to his wife.

"Look, he's moving!" he would shout.

I would of course freeze before she could turn around and spot me in motion. She would give me a glance and turn back to her husband shaking her head.

"The only thing that is going to be moving is me," she would reply. "Knock it off or go take your medication. I just want some peace and quiet so I can read."

"No, look. He was there and now he is over there."

As she shook her head and returned to her book I stood up on my hind legs and looked directly at the man. I even did a small binky to add to my taunting.

He dare not disturb his wife again. He looked at me with angry eyes and shook his head. He knew there was nothing he could do about what I was doing but I knew he was not happy. It was a fun way to spend the afternoon.

SOMETHING IS WRONG

I am not really sure when I started to feel that something was wrong. I just woke up one morning in early October back in Illinois and didn't feel quite right. It is hard to describe because nothing hurt, there was no fever just this fog that had descended upon me.

My body was trying to alert me to some kind of hidden enemy that was invading my body, trying to take control. Maybe it was something that I had eaten. Maybe I had just slept in an odd position the night before. Maybe it was a passing virus. Or maybe it was all just in my head.

For the time being it did not seem to be upsetting my day-to-day routine. I got up and decided that I was going to make the best of it.

But as I struggled to get through the days ahead it was becoming clear that something was seriously wrong and ignoring it was not going to work. This was more than bad food, a bad night of sleep or some bunny bug.

I was losing my appetite. The haze in my mind was spreading like a thick morning fog. It was growing harder and harder to focus. Jumping up on the couch to snag a treat from Roy now felt like trying to scale a 100-foot wall. I tried twice only to come crashing down to the ground. I hopped away to the shelter of the little cardboard house Sharon had made me.

"Do you think he's okay?" Sharon asked. "He isn't making much poop lately and I can see he is not drinking his water."

"Maybe it's just the weather," Roy answered. "You know how he sometimes stops eating for a bit when the weather changes."

He crawled up to my house and reached in to pet me.

"What's wrong in there?"

All I could do was look up. There was no way for me to tell him what was going on. Rabbits don't have the gift of speech so it's kinda hard to tell someone when you are sick.

"Look," Roy said staring at me. "I am going to figure this out.

Sharon, being the good bunny mother she was, knew something was wrong and that it was more than just a change in the weather. She started to monitor everything I did. She wrote down what I ate, what time I ate, how much I ate, how much I drank and how much poop and pee there was in my litter box.

What goes in a bunny must come out. And when nothing comes out of a bunny it means that nothing is going in or that the miraculous processing plant inside all living things is somehow broken.

My condition continued to slide downhill. Foraging for food was getting harder. I had no real desire to drink. I began to feel a small ache in the left side of my body. I was losing the desire to do anything but sleep and lay in the sun.

I knew Covid-19 was causing issues for humans but was not sure if I could catch it. Bunnies have their own list of diseases and I had never heard of this Covid thing. I could see from the TV that a lot of people were wearing masks. Bunnies don't wear masks. It gets in the way of our whiskers.

Finally, after a few days of watching me struggle, Sharon had seen enough.

"I think we need to take him to the vet. Something is not right and I am worried he is a lot sicker than we think."

Roy agreed, but tried to remain reassuring. Now, I am not a big fan of going to the animal doctor as I call him. They always seem to be giving you shots, probing places that should not be probed and squeezing things you don't want squeezed.

But in this case, I was not going to resist. I knew that I was sick and that unless I got some kind of care soon this was not going to end well.

"Still no poop or pee," Roy announced one afternoon after giving my litter box a close exam. "He also isn't eating anything. I think he needs to go in."

"I made an appointment for tomorrow. I think he is starting to lose weight and he just lays around all day."

That night after Sharon went to sleep Roy came over and whispered, "Don't worry little one. You will be okay. We won't let anything bad happen to you."

He laid next to me for several minutes petting my head and then the rest of my body. I slowly fell into a deep sleep.

BAD NEWS

The next morning Sharon loaded me into my carrying case and we were off for inspection. I could tell from the look on her face and her demeanor that she was concerned.

The animal doctor poked and prodded me as he usually did. However, this time I felt a sharp pain in my left side. That was new and it hurt. I jerked and the animal doctor decided the issue required further examination.

I was placed under this giant silver machine that looked like something from another world.

"This will give us a look inside our little friend here to see exactly what is going on," the doctor said as he moved me into position.

The machine let out a series of noises in growing intensity as it began to power up. The whirring noise grew louder and louder followed by a series of clicks. The animal doctor then rolled me over to get pictures from every possible angle.

Out of the corner of my eye, I could see Sharon with a very concerned look on her face. I could tell this was very serious business.

The animal doctor finished his exam and left the room announcing he would return after he took a look at the films he had just taken. We only had to wait a few minutes for him to return but the wait seemed like days.

Without warning, he came up and gave me some kind of shot. I was used to shots but this one caught me off guard. He rubbed my butt where he had placed the injection as if that would somehow make it better.

He then walked over to talk to Sharon who was waiting several feet away. I could not hear what the animal doctor was telling Sharon but the news was clearly not good. She started to cry and I could see that he was trying to comfort her.

They talked for a few more minutes. He handed her a couple of vials of something. Sharon wiped away her tears as she started to write down a series of instructions.

She asked a series of questions and then made some more notes. After a few more minutes she put the paper in her pocket and gave the animal doctor a hug. She came to pick me up and put in back in the carrying case I had come in.

"Don't wait too long," he said. "You don't want him to suffer. This condition could be extremely painful."

"How long?"

"Not long. We are talking a matter of days not weeks. Today is Tuesday. I would say Thursday or Friday at the most. The shot I gave him should relieve some of the pain he may be feeling. It may help kick start his system."

"Thank you," Sharon said.

"Here is our number. Call when it is time."

I wasn't sure exactly what was going on but the news could not be good. Days instead of weeks did not sound good, neither did I think you know when it's time. Time for what?

Sharon got on the phone to call Roy at home.

"We will need to talk when I get home. It's not good," she blurted out as she once again started to cry. "I gotta go."

When we got home, Sharon told Roy the bad news. My left kidney was filled with kidney stones and no longer functioning. That meant I was running on just one kidney which was something bunnies cannot do for long.

The animal doctor had given me some kind of shot to help rehydrate my body and get my one remaining kidney going again. It seemed to be working. I started to feel a bit better and was able to pee for what seemed like the first time in days.

"We need to do what we can to make him feel comfortable," Sharon instructed.

That night Roy gave me pretzels, bananas, apples, extra pellets and all the other things I loved. The extra treats and pets all seemed to give me a brief boost.

For a few days, I felt a little bit better. But I could not shake the fog that had overtaken my brain. I had a hard time foraging for my food. Everything looked strange, nothing smelled right. I would walk into familiar objects, suddenly unaware of the world around me.

I tried to rally but the effort was too much at times. The slightest movement was exhausting. The sole joy I had each day was greeting the sunlight as it came streaming in the doors and windows. It reminded me of my days back on the farm.

Sharon would wake up in the middle of the night to check on me and talk to me. She held me and tried to will me back to health but there was nothing she could do. I was comforted by her rubs and pets. If her love were a medicine I would recover in a manner of minutes. It was breaking my heart that there seemed nothing that could be done to save me.

Roy was defiant about it all. He was not going to give up on me despite what the animal doctor had said. See Roy also had a bad kidney and he thought that if he could survive with broken parts, so could I. He was fond of saying suck it up buttercup. I was about to learn what that meant.

He came home the next day with a giant bag of vegetables he had collected at the local markets around town. There was every imaginable green leafy vegetable you could imagine. Since I had lost my taste for my traditional diet of romaine lettuce, parsley and mixed greens he set out to find a substitute.

His bags were filled with red dandelions, kale, swiss chard, and a long list of other things most people can't pronounce. He would also climb up into the honey locust tree behind the house to cut down branches of the leaves I loved so much.

He had learned much about bunnies over time by observing them in the wild and watching what his house bunnies liked.

Since he knew that I was having a hard time drinking water from the bottles in my cage and the bowls that had been laid out he offered me water from a cup. I found it much easier to drink this way since it required much less effort.

He was quite the sight kneeling to offer a bunny water from a cup, offering foods that might reignite my desire to eat. Love and hope are powerful medicines and I could feel their powers working on me. I started to believe in the magic of it all.

Each day I started to grow a little stronger. Sharon's pets, hugs and words of love started to heal my spirit. Roy's crazy efforts to get me to eat and drink started to do the same for my body.

When Friday came and went, I was still walking planet Earth. I was somehow still alive despite the dire predictions. In fact, I felt pretty good.

Then came Saturday and Sunday. I was still here. I was not surprised. Sharon and Roy were not giving up on me, so I certainly was not going down without a fight. It did make things a bit awkward though. People started to ask how I was doing since my demise had been so imminent, such a sure thing. But it seems there are no sure things in this world, not even death. It was not my time yet, and the rally rabbit was born.

THE RALLY RABBIT

Roy was the one who pinned the Rally Rabbit nickname on me. Since my diagnosis had been so dire and dark, many of their friends had assumed bad news was only a day or two away, perhaps a week at the most.

After two days turned into two weeks one of their friends was bold enough to ask, "How's Werner?"

Many were surprised when Roy wrote them back, saying the Rally Rabbit was indeed alive and doing rather well. I still wasn't quite right but my energy and appetite had returned, though I had a sudden craving for new foods.

Sharon kept a constant check on every piece of poop that came out of me, every drop of pee. She wrote down what I ate, what I drank and even when I slept.

Roy set up feeding and watering stations around the back room where I spent most of my time. While the fog that had clouded my mind had started to partially lift it was still thick enough to impair my ability for forage for food. I sometimes had no idea just where I was and what I was supposed to be doing.

The more I ate the stronger I became. The pain I had been feeling started to subside. Life slowly returned to normal, or as normal as it could be.

Roy and Sharon were starting to once again get ready for their annual trip to Florida. I was anxious to return since I had enjoyed it so much the first time. It was just one week away and I could hear them talking about whether I would survive the trip or even still be around when the time came to leave.

As they packed up their bags and containers, I could see they were making plans to take me along. I could see a whole box marked Werner and it was filled with my stuff. It is a luxury all bunnies enjoy when they travel. Their human masters pack for them and carry their stuff. It makes you feel like a rock star.

Roy had thought about sending me down on a plane with Sharon. I had seen planes fly overhead from time to time. I thought them nothing but human madness. Birds flew, humans should not. Birds had wings for flight, humans had legs for walking.

Sharon had put a quick end to the discussion saying that a flight would not be a good idea. We would drive. That was fine with me for it meant lots of food, water, treats and plenty of sleep.

It was still dark when they loaded me into my cage and a waiting car. It was late October and the air was brisk with the first bite of winter wind that was to come. We would be long gone before the worst of it arrived.

We arrived in Florida and the warmth there was great relief to my aching bones. 16 hours in a car is a long time for any creature, even a bunny. You can only take so many hours of the Beatles' greatest hits, Roy's Rammstein racket and Sharon's Coffee House tunes. The endless drone of the road was sometimes a pleasant relief.

After we unpacked and got set up in our condo the countdown to the various holidays began. The first to arrive was Halloween. It was another goofy human custom I did not understand. Human children would dress up as various creatures and characters and then go out and beg for candy. I had heard the holiday was created to ward off the ghosts of the dead. I was not aware the dead were really walking around. It was strange but it seemed to make everyone happy.

Once Halloween had passed and the leftover candy was gone, all attention turned to Thanksgiving. Thanksgiving seemed to be a day for eating, watching football, drinking and family fights that often led to great drama and days of regret and apologies.

I was most thankful for my nice home and the fact I was a rabbit. This was not a good day for turkeys. Being a rabbit was a very good thing on Thanksgiving. People came over to play with me, not eat me.

Thanksgiving didn't end before I could hear people start to talk about

Christmas. I was supposed to be about the birth of this baby humans called Jesus but it seemed to be more about them running out to buy things.

It seemed the humans would buy themselves things know that the gifts they would get from others would be a disappointment. I would watch as Sharon and Roy would open presents at various Christmas gatherings and feign wonder. Yet a few days later I would find many of those gifts either in the trash or in my pen so that I could chew on them.

For a holiday with such a buildup it seemed to leave many people sad and angry. I would hear a lot of words animals do not use to describe the gifts and the people who gave them.

Animals do not exchange gifts. We are what we are every day and treat each day with equal respect. We do not need special days to gather or perform acts of kindness. After all, you cannot buy the greatest gifts in any store at any price. For the greatest gifts are life itself, love, hope and the respect we show all we encounter.

I had often thought that maybe humans should get rid of all of their holidays and spend more time just being nice to each other. They might be better off. They seemed to spend too much time preparing for holidays that just left them feeling sad and alone. They seemed to spend too much time on things, not enough on each other and the things that really mattered.

I survived to see the new year arrive. It is a time of new hope and new beginnings. Something told me this would be my last new year. Even though I was feeling pretty good I knew time was not on my side. The time I had been given would eventually run out.

January was awesome. The warm days gave way to cool nights which bunnies love. During the day I would nap in the sun. At night I would perch on the lanai and listen to all of the animals prowling the night. It was a hidden symphony only I could hear.

I was enjoying my home in Florida. There was a lot of rehab work going on which meant lots of boxes to play in and chew on. It also meant lots of carry-out junk food and plenty of crumbs to feast on.

I learned that I did not care much for Chinese food but much enjoyed the crumbs from fried chicken and tiny pieces of French fries that fell my way. Occasionally, there would be a morsel or two of Coleslaw. It became one of my favorites. Of course, I would binky every time some potato chips or pretzels would fall my way.

In the early days of February, I could start to feel the call every living creature eventually feels. It is the call of the Creator letting you know to prepare for the passage. The love of Sharon and Roy and my will was simply not going to be enough for me to go on much longer.

My body started to send me a new warning. This time it was my heart and there would be no reprieve, no rally from this. It began to beat in irregularly, making it difficult for me to breathe or move at times.

The episodes would often leave as quickly as they came but each one was more intense, more disruptive.

Roy was the first to notice one night after Sharon went to sleep. He noticed my heart beating rapidly through my fur. When I did not answer his call to come over to get a treat, he sensed that something was very wrong.

He picked me up and offered me a treat but I had no interest. I felt disoriented and confused by what was happening to me. I had trouble breathing and looked at Roy. He immediately knew that my light was slowly fading. This would be the final road home. I could feel the tears fall onto my fur as he hugged me.

"That's okay, little one. Maybe tomorrow. For now, Sharon does not need to know. Let's give her another day before we give her this news. Let her enjoy her rally rabbit for as long as she can."

The next morning, I realized days could now be a matter of hours. I was unable to move very far and breathing was a chore. I was embarrassed to find I could not reach my litter box. When Sharon discovered my condition, she became alarmed.

"He's not eating," Sharon announced. "I think this might be it. I want to take him back to the vet."

Roy nodded and before I knew it, I was off to the animal doctor once more. He only confirmed what we all already knew. My time had come.

"He has congestive heart failure," Sharon murmured to Roy when she returned home. "There is nothing they can do this time. The vet says make him comfortable. Give him anything he wants."

"That's it?" Roy protested.

"Yes. We have taken him as far as we can go. We cannot let him suffer. There are no more miracles to be had, no more rallies. He could last three or four more days but they would be painful and we do not want that."

Roy nodded. It was the first time I could sense the defeat in his spirit. Sharon's eyes filled with tears and they held each other. They picked me up and brought me in.

"I am so sorry," Sharon whispered. "You are such a good bunny."

The memories of all the crazy times I had shared with them now came flooding back. The times I have been caught eating wires or shoes. The times they had laughed at me for stopping to watch movies on TV that I enjoyed. The times I had jumped up on the couch seeking a piece of pizza, some ice cream or some other treat. The times I was sound asleep on the floor moving wildly around as I had bunny dreams of swimming, running and flying.

They joked about how even after I was gone there would be memories of me everywhere. I had chewed on every hat Roy owned. I had munched on half the books Sharon owned. Many of the lights in the house would flicker on because of the nibbles I left behind.

We all knew that it was time for me to go home. Sharon and Roy knew it was their job now to get me there. I could hear them talking about making sure I was not cheated of one moment of life. Always they talked about making sure they did not want me to suffer.

It is tough to let go of something you love. It goes against the basic instinct every living being has to cling to life to the very end. But it can be selfish to hang on to it when the Creator decides it is time for you to return home.

I spent a large part of my final full day basking in the sun. I thought about my life, my parents, my brothers and sisters and all the grand things I had seen.

I thought about how I would miss Sharon and Roy. I could see how my struggle was causing them such pain. I wanted so much to let them know it was okay, that it was my time. But I was too weak, too tired.

The sun went down and darkness returned. Sharon stayed by my side, petting my head, kissing me and whispering kind words. Roy would take over when she needed a break, offering me a treat. I could only look up with sadness that those days had passed.

Breathing was becoming more and more difficult. My heart beat was growing more and more erratic and uncomfortable. As each episode came, I worried it would be the last. My spirit was preparing for the end.

I knew I was now approaching the moment every living being must face, the point where you pass from this living world into whatever lies beyond.

I did not sleep my final night. I could not find a comfortable position to lay in. My heart was also beating so loudly and my breathing was so labored that it was hard to hear anything else. I would gasp for air and then calm myself when I caught a breath. I then lie there waiting for the next wave to hit.

I knew the time had come where hours would turn into minutes and then moments. I could sense the sun would rise soon and my final wish would be to bask one more day in its light. I so longed for one more day in the sun.

Just as dawn was about to break, Roy came in to cover me with his favorite green shirt. He somehow knew that I was cold. The shirt was special because he wore it at the horse rescue where he and Sharon did volunteer work. It was a place where they took care of abused and abandoned horses.

"Here my little friend," he said placing the shirt over me.

"This will help. This is my magic shirt. It makes me feel better when I am down. We are here. We will take care of you."

He stayed with me until Sharon arrived and took his place. I could hear her tears falling on the wood floor where I was laying. It was like rain falling from the sky.

My heart was now splitting open with pain, not from any physical problem but from the sadness I felt. The sadness I would soon be leaving this world behind. Soon be leaving those who loved me so much.

I could soon see the first emissaries of the sunlight struggle to crawl over the horizon. I could not move so Roy picked me up and placed me in a spot where the sun would soon reach me. He somehow knew my final wish.

I watched as the rays of the sun inched closer and closer to me. I could feel the light inside me fade as the light outside grew stronger.

The sunlight soon enveloped me in a peaceful hug. I could feel the presence of all living things around me and all that had come before me. Its peace and warmth gave me the strength to cross the Rainbow Bridge every rabbit must eventually pass over.

After a few more pets and hugs, Sharon whispered, "It's time to go."

Sharon picked me up for the final time and carried me to the car. There would be no cage, no carrying case this time. I was safely in her arms, no place else I would rather be.

Roy drove as they talked once more about whether they were doing the right thing. They were convinced it was time and waiting would only bring more suffering to me.

Their love, the comfort of the sun, memories of my parents and a presence I cannot describe made feel me ready for the journey ahead. It was my time. I was afraid of what was to come as we all are because it is so uncertain. I also mourned for what I had to leave behind.

Sharon held me as the animal doctor came into the room I had seen all too frequently in the past few months. He was not laughing and joking as he normally did. We all knew this was a moment for respect and honor.

"This is the right thing," he said. You do not want him to suffer anymore."

Sharon and Roy were now both trying to hold back tears. They were not doing a very good job of it.

"I love you so much," Sharon whispered.

"We will miss you," Roy added.

And with that, I took a final breath and fell into a deep sleep. The reality of the world slipped away. First, the light faded and then the sound. I could no longer feel my heart beat or my lungs taking a breath. Soon, there was no sense of anything.

I had often heard Sharon talk of the Rainbow Bridge that all bunnies passed over when they died. But I was never sure whether it was true or not. Bunnies do not often have the time or opportunity to discuss such grand matters.

Now, here I was, standing in front of a grand wooden bridge. It was pristine in appearance, a solid brown oak. Every plank was perfectly cut, every bolt and nail in a meticulous straight line. The railings were straight and true designed to direct creatures big and small across the large creek that run below it.

The water in the creek was a perfect aqua blue. I could see fish, turtles, frogs and all manner of other creatures swimming about. They were swimming in and out of amazing green beds of plants that covered the bottom and red and yellow Lily pads that floated on top.

The water was so clear that you could see every pebble and rock that covered the bottom. Ducks swam on top and birds drank from its fresh waters from along the banks.

Across the bridge, I could see not one but two rainbows lighting the sky. The clouds were a brilliant white and, in all shapes, and sizes. The sun bathed the world below in a peaceful golden light. The landscape was covered in a carpet of trees, flowers and all manner of plants that created a colorful quilt.

I turned around to look behind me but saw nothing but cold, infinite darkness. It was not clear if I had passed through it to arrive at the foot of the bridge or had been transported here some other way. It was clearly not the direction I wanted to travel.

I decided that I would go forward to cross the bridge, if and when the courage came. The landscape before me was brilliant and alive with the sounds of life.

A gust of wind passed through me and I was suddenly aware that I was once again breathing and that my heart was beating. The pain I had been suffering was now gone. The fog that had clouded my final days had lifted.

I took a cleansing breath and summoned the courage to take the first steps toward this new world. The cold and darkness behind me began to fade as the light and warmth took control.

About halfway across the bridge, I could make out a figure on the other side. It was shrouded in a mist at first. As I drew closer, I could see that it was a small tree.

"Welcome," it said.

"Hello," I replied in amazement. "Who are you? I have never met a talking tree before."

"Well, that is because you have never taken the time to listen. All living things have a voice, you simply need to be quiet, listen and allow them to speak. Here you will find a great many things you have not seen or heard before."

"What is your name?"

"I am Samuel. And you are Werner. We have been expecting you for some time. The love from the last world has brought you here."

"What is this place?"

"This place is whatever you can imagine, whatever you want to make it. It is a place of love, of hope and of creation. This is the world beyond the Rainbow Bridge."

"So, it's real?"

"Of course, it is."

"I thought it was just a tale, that…."

"I can assure you it is very much real."

"What happens to me now?"

"That is up to you. You shall decide."

"Where will I live?"

"Wherever you wish to make a home. The land here is endless."

"Can I ask what happened to Sharon and Roy? How are they doing? I feel bad that I left them behind."

"Are you sure you want to see? It can be difficult."

"Yes."

"Close your eyes."

I closed my eyes and could feel the tree envelop me in its branches. It felt warm and safe.

My head immediately filled with a vision of Sharon and Roy. Sharon was holding my lifeless body. Roy was nearby digging a hole. They were at the horse rescue, a place that had given them great comfort.

Matt and Tina, the people who ran the rescue, had welcomed them with open arms when they asked to place me there. They said it would be an honor to have another gentle soul join the spirits there.

Samuel began to tell me what I was seeing, "Roy believed it was sacred ground because of all the horses that were cared for there. Horses that had been pulled from the edge of darkness, from abuse and neglect. They now run free in the sunlight again to enjoy their final days. Some will join us soon, others when their time comes."

"This is called Joker's Field. It is named after Joker, a horse who is buried there. This field is well known to us as a passage point for animals who need a final home. You will find many of them here as you travel."

I watched as Roy carefully took my body and lowered it into the ground. I was facing toward the east. The direction the sun rose in every day. I would face the sun every day it came up just as I had when I was with them.

They chose a spot under some trees in the field. The horses there would watch over their little friend and the others who had passed for as long as they walked and grazed the land.

I was wrapped in a beautiful white towel as Roy gently lowered me into the ground. He took great care in making sure my body was placed in just the right spot. He caressed my body for a final time before covering my face with the towel. Sharon cried. Roy fought back tears. He did not do a very good job of it.

The horses in the nearby paddocks came to attention for the ceremony to stand as witnesses, watching me pass from one world to the next. They bowed their majestic heads in respect as my body was covered with the gentle, sweet Earth.

When they were finished filling the hole, they put a small wooden cross on my grave that Roy had made. Sharon wrote a little message on it that reads, "Crossing the Rainbow Bridge. Werner. 2-4-21."

"Do you want to go on?"

"Yes."

I continued to watch as they said a little prayer and asked the horses on the other side to watch over me.

As the days passed Roy made a little book of photos as a reminder of the time I had spent with them. Sharon took my passing hard and Roy bought her a stuffed bunny to help ease her pain. They were shocked when it arrived and looked just like me.

It is amazing how such a tiny life, such a small being can touch so many lives, even inspire people. A volunteer at the horse rescue by the name of Carolyn heard my story. She had recently taken a few painting lessons. Sharon asked if she could create a painting of me. I do not know who guided her hand but my portrait is her first work and it graces the cover of this book. It is a masterpiece in my eye.

It was all a reminder of how much I was loved. And it is also a reminder that life does go on.

The final images the tree allowed me to see are those of a baby Sandhill Crane which now wanders the horse rescue. A pair of cranes had roamed the rescue for some days before I died. Then suddenly one disappeared. With all of the predators roaming this Florida land, everyone thought the worst.

Yet, just days after I left the mother crane returned, with a brand-new baby at her side. The family of three now roams the rescue. New life.

Not long after that, there are imagines of Roy mowing the grass coming across a Killdeer, a small bird. She was guarding two eggs that will soon hatch. And there are the baby bunnies, frogs, snakes and birds which all call this sacred place home. It is much more than a rescue; it is a sanctuary of life.

If you do not believe there are special places on this earth where miracles happen you must simply go out and look because they are all around you. Perhaps we do not realize until it is too late just how precious life is, how amazing each day in the sun can be.

I can see that Sharon and Roy now have a new bunny to care for. His name is Peanut and just like me, he was rescued from the wilderness and then from death in a cold room. He was dumped into a field and rescued by a woman before alligators or eagles or other predators could snatch him up.

He is the runt of his litter, with odd stick legs and a crazy personality. But he was grabbed from the edge of darkness, just like I was, just like the horses at the rescue where my body now lies. But he is bringing the joy back to Sharon and Roy doing the things bunnies do.

He eats wires, just like I did. He loves his snacks, just like I did. He likes to sleep inside the couch, just like I did. And he does other things I did not, like flipping over backward like an idiot trying to pick up a bowl. And he loves to be given pets, hugs and kisses, just like I did. He is in good hands.

"Thank you," I said. "I have seen enough. I feel much better now."

"Good. I think you have learned that you live on as long as others remember you in their hearts, their memories and their dreams. Know that you will never be forgotten as long as your name is spoken, your memories cherished."

I look in from time to time on Sharon and Roy. I see them visit the place where I rest. Roy came to talk about my book and helped me write some of it. I watch and laugh as they create new adventures and memories with Peanut.

The tears and pain of my final days have now been replaced with laughs and grand tales of adventure over the things we did together. I am remembered as a mythical creature of immense stature. People smile when they hear my name. It is the best gift I could ask for.

Life does indeed go on and each one of us needs to remember that every day is precious. You are only given so many days in the sun. You can use them to create grand moments and memories or spend them in ill pursuit.

Don't wait until your last day in the sun to wonder what you did with all the others. Let your heart bathe in the happiness and joy of your life. When you stand before the Rainbow Bridge, as we all shall do someday, know your life had meaning.

Printed in Great Britain
by Amazon

22436836R00089